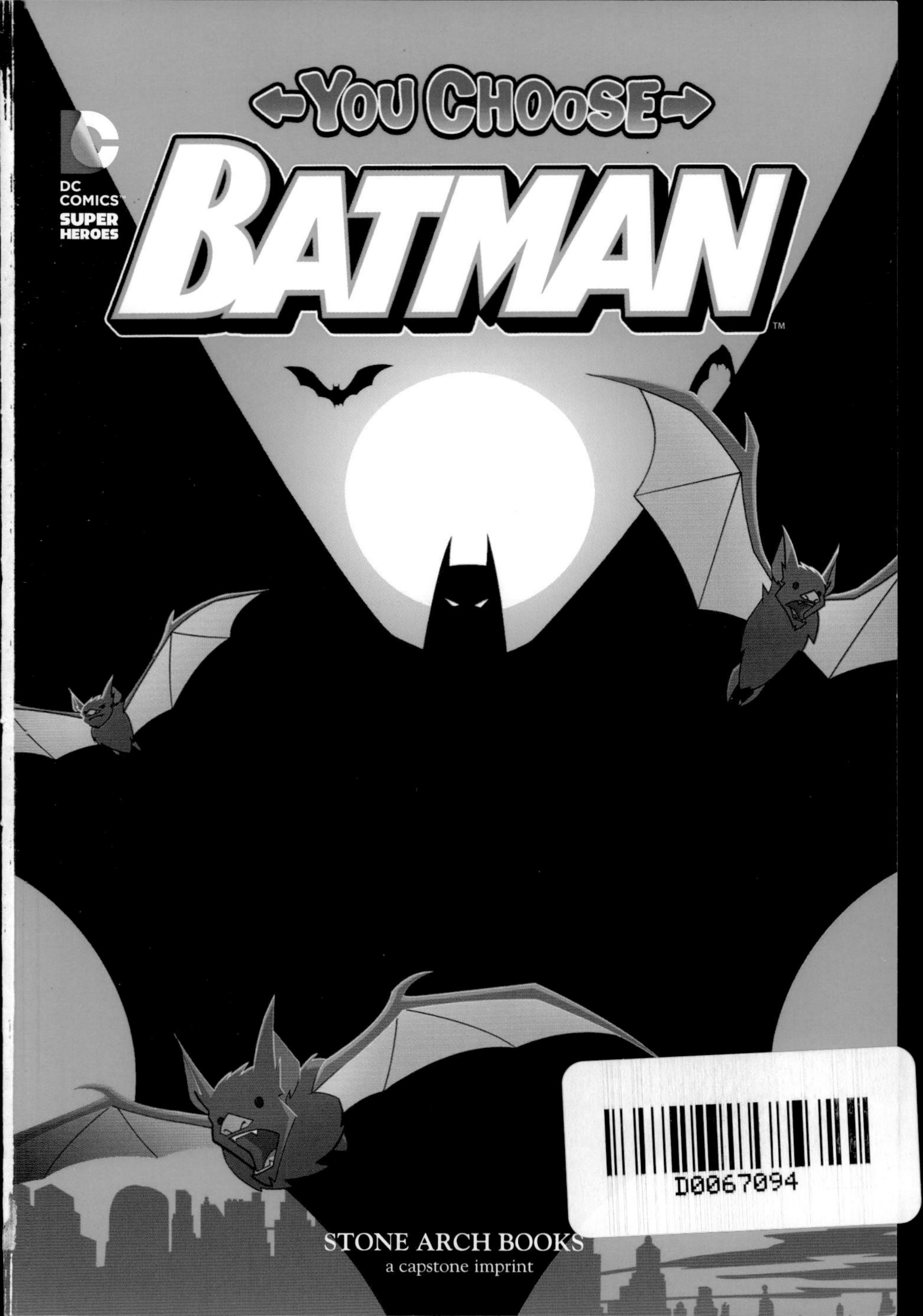
YOU CHOOSE
BATMAN™
DC COMICS™
SUPER HEROES
STONE ARCH BOOKS
a capstone imprint

You Choose Stories: Batman
is published by Stone Arch Books,
A Capstone Imprint
1710 Roe Crest Drive
North Mankato, Minnesota 56003
www.capstonepub.com

STAR34128

Cataloging-in-Publication Data is available
on the Library of Congress website.
ISBN: 978-1-4965-0529-3 (library binding)
ISBN: 978-1-4965-0531-6 (paperback)
ISBN: 978-1-4965-2306-8 (eBook)

Summary: It's a triple threat! Catwoman, Poison Ivy, and
Harley Quinn have crashed a charity fundraiser and made
off with all the cash. With your help, he'll solve the puzzle
of The Terrible Trio!

Printed in the United States of America in North Mankato, Minnesota.
042016   009710R

DC COMICS™
SUPER
HEROES

←◆ YOU CHOOSE ◆→

BATMAN™

THE
TERRIBLE
TRIO

Batman created by Bob Kane

written by
Laurie S. Sutton

illustrated by
Ethen Beavers

←YOU CHOOSE→
BATMAN
™

It's a triple threat! Catwoman, Poison Ivy, and
Harley Quinn have crashed a charity fundraiser
and made off with all the cash. With your help,
he'll solve the puzzle of *The Terrible Trio*!

Follow the directions at the bottom of each
page. The choices YOU make will change the
outcome of the story. After you finish one path,
go back and read the others for more Batman
adventures!

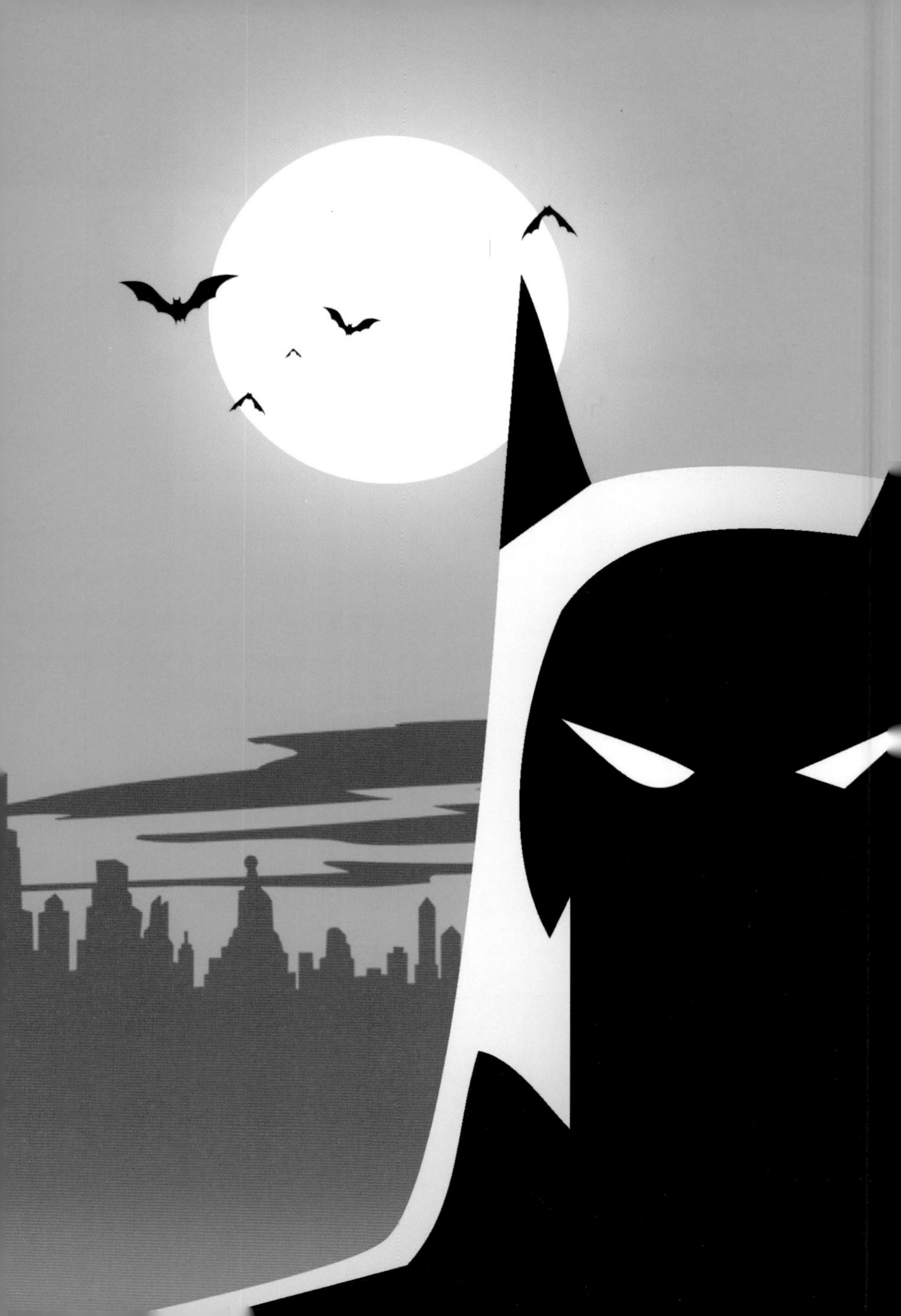

Bruce Wayne looks at crowd of party guests and wishes he were fighting crime as Batman.

He stands on the balcony at one end of a ballroom inside the private Gotham City Adventurers Club. The hall is filled with animal trophies and unusual objects brought back from trips to far-off lands. Potted plants have been brought in to make the room look like a jungle. In the center of the ballroom is a bowl shaped like a tiger. Its stripes are made of gold and black diamonds. Its green eyes are giant emeralds. The bowl is brimming with cash and checks.

"Thank you for your generous donation, Bruce," a woman says as she walks up to Bruce Wayne. She is dressed in a fancy gown.

"This party is for a good cause, and I want to help the endangered tigers and the vanishing jungles of the world," Bruce replies.

Turn the page.

"Help!" someone yells from the floor below.

From up on the balcony, Bruce Wayne can see who has cried out — and why! The shout is from an older gentleman who has been pushed off his feet by a costumed criminal dressed like a jester.

"Outta the way, grandpa!" the crook demands.

The man falls into one of the potted plants. It turns out to be the safest place to be, because right behind the jester are two more outlaws. Bruce Wayne recognizes all three felons. As Batman, he has fought them many times.

"Harley Quinn, Poison Ivy, and Catwoman!" Bruce gasps.

"Bruce! What's happening?" the woman next to him asks, grabbing his arm in fear.

"Stay here. Call the police!" Bruce instructs as he twists from her grip and runs toward the exit.

Bruce Wayne hurries down the back stairs of the Adventurers Club three steps at a time. He can hear the screams of the party guests behind him in the ballroom.

"Alfred, I need a change of clothes," Bruce whispers into a communications device built into his watch.

"Understood, Master Bruce," replies Alfred Pennyworth, Bruce Wayne's loyal butler.

As Bruce exits the building, he sees Alfred waiting for him with the Wayne limo. The back door pops open. A Batman costume is spread out on the backseat. Bruce Wayne nods his thanks and enters the limo.

It's Batman who exits.

The Dark Knight sprints back into the Adventurers Club. When he gets to the ballroom, it looks like a rain forest has sprouted indoors. The potted palms have grown to gigantic heights. Ivy vines look more like pythons than houseplants.

Batman pushes through the jungle and confronts the villainous trio.

"I won't let you rob this worthy cause," the Dark Knight declares.

Turn the page.

Batman throws a Batarang at Catwoman to stop her from stealing the gold-and-diamond tiger bowl full of cash. *THWAAKK!* The Batarang smacks into Catwoman's fingers and makes her drop the valuable bowl.

"Owww! I'm not stealing. I'm taking this money to make sure it's used to protect the tigers," Catwoman protests.

Suddenly an overgrown ivy vine snatches the bowl before it hits the floor. Batman watches as the container is lifted into the air and shakes its contents of cash into a giant flower blossom. The vine returns the tiger bowl to Catwoman.

"So am I," Poison Ivy says. "I don't trust these people to save the vanishing jungles. All they want is an excuse for a party."

"Party! Party! Party!" Harley Quinn whoops as she snatches diamond jewelry from the guests. "I just want the sparkly things!"

"You know I have to stop you," Batman states.

The Dark Knight hurls a Batrope at Harley.

The wire wraps around her like a straitjacket. Then Batman pulls a small sphere from his Utility Belt and tosses it at Catwoman.

PWOOF! Sleep gas sprays out.

"You're a clever bat," Poison Ivy admits.

"And you're next," the Dark Knight promises.

"I don't think so," Ivy declares.

Suddenly a potted fern extends its fronds to tangle around Batman. As he struggles to get free, he sees Catwoman stumble up the stairs to the balcony and Harley escape from the Batrope.

"You know I must stop you," Batman repeats.

RIIIP! Batman uses his strength to shred the strangling ferns holding him.

"Split up!" Ivy shouts to her fellow felons. "He can't chase all of us at once!"

The trio of costumed criminals flees in separate directions!

If Batman goes after Catwoman, turn to page 12.
If Batman pursues Poison Ivy, turn to page 14.
If Batman chases Harley Quinn, turn to page 16.

Batman watches the partners in crime run away in separate directions. He can go after only one, and he chooses to pursue Catwoman. She has the priceless tiger bowl!

Catwoman is groggy from the sleeping gas. She stumbles up the stairs toward the ballroom balcony. The Dark Knight hurls a Batarang at the fleeing feline felon.

THWUUUNK! The Batarang knocks the bowl from Catwoman's grasp. As she automatically stops to grab it, Batman runs up the last few steps and catches up to her.

"Hand over the bowl and surrender," the Dark Knight suggests.

"How about a deal?" Catwoman grins and throws the tiger bowl into the air. "You get the bowl, and I don't surrender!"

Batman lunges at Catwoman as she runs away, but he catches the tiger instead of the cat. He puts the bowl on the floor and continues the chase.

Suddenly, Batman hears breaking glass. He follows the sound to a smashed skylight at the top of the Adventurers Club. Batman climbs out of the opening and spots Catwoman running across the roof. He fires a Batrope after the fleeing feline. It misses her!

"Bats *are* blind!" Catwoman laughs.

The Batrope wraps around one of the flagpoles at the edge of the roof. Batman tugs on the rope, and the flagpole topples toward Catwoman. She doesn't realize her downfall until she's tangled up in the flag fabric.

"I wasn't aiming for you," Batman reveals as he walks toward the wrapped-up wrongdoer. He takes out a pair of Bat-cuffs.

"You can't cage this kitty!" Catwoman hisses as she uses her claws to rip her way out. She perches on the edge of the roof and then leaps.

Batman jumps after her. He doesn't expect what happens next!

If Batman lands on the roof of a speeding train, turn to page 18.
If a giant vine grabs the Dark Knight, turn to page 25.

As the partners in crime split up, Batman turns to face Poison Ivy with a pair of Bat-cuffs in his hand.

"Surrender and there won't be any trouble," the Dark Knight says.

"Oh, there will be trouble," Ivy promises.

The Queen of Green waves her arms and all the plants in the place grow to enormous size. They bend and weave together to form a giant carpet of vegetation under her feet. It lifts her off the floor. Ivy points at a party guest, and a thick vine snatches him off his feet.

"Heeelp!" the man yells as he is enclosed in a huge flower blossom.

The immense plant platform suddenly sprouts roots that look like centipede legs. It scurries out of the building and into the streets of Gotham City. **SCREEEECH!** Traffic skids and swerves.

Batman fires a his grapnel and hitches a ride on Ivy's mutant chariot. **SWWOOOSH! WHOOOSH!** Vines whip all around him.

The Caped Crusader uses his acrobatic skills to tumble and roll to avoid the tendrils. His focus is on Poison Ivy.

SMAAAACK! Batman tackles her and knocks her off the platform. It continues to crawl forward even without her.

"You can't stop me, Batman," Ivy boasts.

"Oh, I will stop you," the Dark Knight promises.

Suddenly a silly-sounding horn honks at them. *BEEEP! BEEEEEEP!* A crazy-looking car drives straight toward Ivy and the Caped Crusader. The driver is Harley Quinn! Batman realizes that both he and Ivy are in danger of being hit. He pushes his foe out of the way, but now he is directly in the path of the madcap car!

The Dark Knight leaps onto the roof of a nearby taxi and escapes. He looks around for Ivy as Harley zooms down the street.

Ivy's gone, but where? Batman wonders.

If Batman sees Poison Ivy running after her plant platform, turn to page 20.

If Batman realizes Ivy is escaping with Harley, turn to page 27.

Batman chases after the closest costumed criminal — Harley Quinn! They run out of the Adventurers Club and down the front stairs. Batman reaches into his Utility Belt and pulls out a Batarang. Harley jumps into a weird-looking car and zooms away before he can throw it.

"She had her getaway planned," the Dark Knight observes. "Well, I planned ahead, too."

Batman takes a remote control from his Utility Belt and presses a button. A car parked across the street transforms into the Batmobile! The Dark Knight slides in behind the wheel and takes off in pursuit of Harley.

Her vehicle is easy to spot. It's the one that looks like a roller-coaster car driving in a crazy zigzag through the evening traffic. Batman has to stop Harley before she hurts someone!

The Dark Knight fires his grapnel at the fleeing car, but Harley swerves at the last second. The Mistress of Mayhem responds by squirting an oil slick at the Batmobile. Batman avoids the danger and continues to follow her.

"I've got to shake that Bat," Harley grumbles.

She heads toward a construction zone.

SMAAAASH! She crashes through a warning barrier. Batman follows. She drives through an obstacle course of dump trucks and construction cranes. Batman follows.

The Dark Knight fires a barrage of caltrops. The sharp spikes stick in one of Harley's tires. **PFFFFT!** It starts to deflate. **FLAP! FLAP! FLAP!** The sound makes Harley laugh!

"Hahaha! That's so funny!" Harley howls.

She's so busy laughing that she drives down a subway entrance. The large Batmobile cannot follow. But there are only two places the subway goes: the fairgrounds or Gotham Seaport.

Batman must choose which direction to follow.

If Batman heads for Gotham Seaport, turn to page 23.
If Batman goes to the fairgrounds, turn to page 29.

Catwoman jumps off the roof of the Adventurers Club, and so does Batman. He already has a Batrope in his hands and is ready to use it to control his leap. He never gets a chance to use it.

An elevated subway train roars along its tracks not far below the Dark Knight. He barely has time to react! Batman grabs the ends of his cape and uses it like a parachute to slow his fall. The Caped Crusader knows he has to time his landing just right!

THUMP! Batman's boots land on the roof of the train.

"I guess bats can land on all fours, too," Catwoman says as she runs along the top of the passenger cars.

Batman chases her to the end of the last car. There is nowhere else to go.

"The train's moving too fast to jump. Surrender and you'll be safe," the Dark Knight says.

"I like living dangerously," Catwoman declares as she lunges at Batman with her sharp claws.

She swipes at the super hero just as the train banks into a curve and throws her off balance.

She begins to fall off the train! The Caped Crusader grabs Catwoman by her wrist and pulls her to safety. She looks at him in surprise.

"Thanks," she says, resuming her attack on her archenemy.

SCREEEEECH! Suddenly the train brakes hard as it approaches a station. Now it's Batman's turn to lose his balance and tip over the edge of the train. Catwoman strikes out with her claws!

Catwoman snags Batman by his Utility Belt and pulls him back to his feet.

"I guess we're even," he says.

Catwoman grins and jumps off the train as it stops at the station.

If Batman chases Catwoman into the Champion Cat Show, turn to page 32.

If Batman sees Catwoman jump into Harley Quinn's car, turn to page 48.

Batman stands on the top of a Gotham City taxi and looks around for Poison Ivy.

"I just saved her from being run over by her partner in crime. A simple thank-you would be nice," the Dark Knight sighs.

"Thaaaank yooou!" a distant voice calls.

Batman spots Poison Ivy running down the street after her plant platform. It's moving toward Gotham Park. The Dark Knight knows that once Ivy reaches the millions of trees and plants in the park it will be impossible to defeat her. She is called the Queen of Green for a good reason.

"I have to stop her at all costs. It's time for desperate action," Batman decides as he pulls a special capsule from his Utility Belt.

The Dark Knight fires a Batrope and swings above Ivy and the street. He throws the capsule onto the pavement between Poison Ivy and her plant platform.

BWAAAAM! The street explodes!

Turn to page 22.

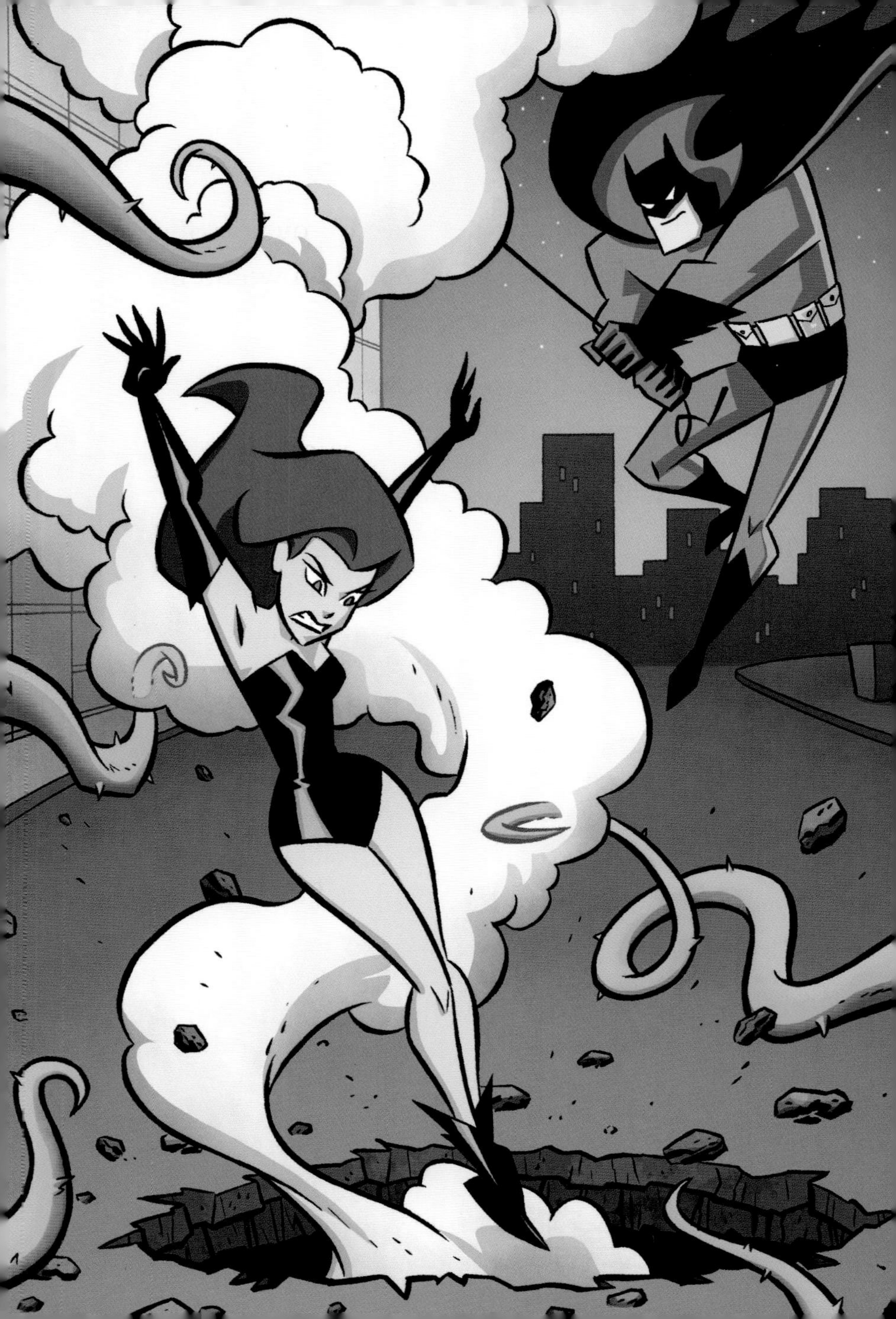

A giant hole opens up in the pavement in front of Poison Ivy. She's not hurt, but she is blocked from reaching her plant platform. She reaches out for a vine to grab her, but suddenly the street collapses under her feet.

Poison Ivy falls into the dark hole. Batman sees her disappear and dives after her!

He lands in a large, underground drainage pipe. There is water up to his ankles. The air smells yucky. Slime grows on the sides of the large pipe. Batman notices that it's glowing!

"She used the plant slime to light her way," Batman concludes as he follows Ivy's illuminated handprints.

The trail leads to a T-junction in the pipe. Then it ends! Batman has a simple choice — go left or right.

But which choice does the Dark Knight make?

If Batman spots a clue in the left-hand tunnel, go to page 34.
If Batman searches the right-hand branch, turn to page 52.

The Dark Knight decides that Harley will go to Gotham Seaport. It's the closest exit from the subway. He knows he has to get there first, and the fastest way is by boat. But not just any boat!

Batman speaks some voice commands into the Batmobile's computer as he drives toward the Gotham River. When he arrives, he steps hard on the Batmobile's brakes and presses the Eject button. The Dark Knight sails through the air and out over the water of the river!

Batman makes a perfect landing in the cockpit of the Batboat. He pushes the throttle to full. *VROOOOM!* The powerful speedboat slices through the water. It doesn't take long before he can see the bright lights of the Seaport. It is a popular spot for Gotham's citizens to shop, dine, and walk. Batman knows the boardwalk will be crowded tonight. People will be in danger from madcap Harley Quinn.

The Batboat arrives at the Seaport, and Batman leaps onto the main pier. He runs through the startled crowds toward the subway.

Turn the page.

When he reaches the entrance, he hears the sounds of squealing tires and people screaming inside the station. He starts to run down the stairs. He stops when he sees Harley's roller-coaster car coming *up* the stairs!

The Dark Knight leaps out of the way and lands on the hood of Harley's vehicle. The Mistress of Mayhem tries to shake him off but only ends up crashing through food stalls and souvenir stands.

"This is no fun. I'm outta here," Harley declares, jumping out of the vehicle.

Batman leaps into the driver's seat and stops the car, but Harley escapes. Or does she? There are two places she can go: into the shopping arcade or onto a dinner-cruise ship.

Batman must decide which way to go!

If Batman chooses to search the shopping arcade, turn to page 36.

If Batman sees Harley on the cruise ship, turn to page 55.

Batman leaps off the roof of the Adventurers Club in pursuit of Catwoman. She is fearless about jumping into thin air, but so is he.

As they both fall toward the pavement below, the Dark Knight can see that Catwoman is aiming toward a horizontal flagpole anchored to the building across the street. He can tell that she is going to grab it and use it to swing to the awning below. Batman has his grapnel in his hand and plans to make a similar move.

Suddenly a giant ivy vine twists up from below and grabs Catwoman in midair. A second vine twirls up and grabs him, too.

"Poison Ivy!" Batman says.

Ivy stands on the sidewalk and gestures at the vine holding Catwoman. The tendril bursts into bloom and gently lowers her to the ground. The vine around Batman begins to tighten.

Batman pulls a Batarang from his Utility Belt and uses the sharp points to saw through the vine. The tendril starts to wither. Batman drops safely to the ground near Catwoman and Ivy.

Turn the page.

They look at each other and run!

Batman fires a Batrope toward a statue on a nearby building. The rope wraps around it, and the Dark Knight swings over the heads of the fleeing felons. He lands in front of them, blocking their escape.

HONK! HONK! Suddenly a horn blares. Headlights speed toward the trio.

Batman is forced to leap aside as a city bus zooms past him. As soon as it passes, Batman notices that Catwoman and Ivy are gone. He sees them on the top of the bus! They wave goodbye.

But Batman reads the route number. There are only two more stops: the Gotham Botanical Gardens and Aqualandia Water Park.

Batman must choose where he thinks they will go.

If Batman decides they will go to the Botanical Gardens, turn to page 68.

If Batman chooses to head for Aqualandia, turn to page 86.

The Dark Knight stands on top of a taxi. *BEEEP! BEEEP!* Harley Quinn honks and drives away in her crazy-looking car.

"Bye-bye, Batman!" Ivy shouts from the passenger seat of Harley's vehicle. She waves and blows a kiss toward the caped crime fighter.

The car speeds down the street toward Ivy's giant green carpet as it crawls toward Gotham Park. The Dark Knight is about to head after it with a Batrope, but a motorcycle cop zooms up to him.

"Hop on!" the officer offers.

The Dark Knight accepts the invitation.

VROOOOM! The motorcycle revs its powerful engine and accelerates after the plant platform. The police officer zigzags through traffic with lights flashing and siren screaming.

WHEEEE-OOOH! WHEEEE-OOOH!

The motorcycle is fast, but not fast enough. A giant vine extends from the platform, grabs Harley's car, and lifts it aboard.

Turn the page.

Poison Ivy stands on the living platform as it enters Gotham Park. She raises her arms like a queen commanding her subjects. The trees bow their branches toward her. They weave their limbs together to form a dense barrier.

"The gates to my realm are closed!" Ivy says.

The motorcycle officer brakes hard when he faces the wall of wood.

SCREEECH! Batman leaps off the back of the cycle and starts to climb the tapestry of tangled branches. The officer tries to follow but keeps slipping back. He watches Batman ascend.

How does he do that? the officer wonders with awe.

The Dark Knight works his way up until he finds a small opening. It's just large enough for him to get through. He wiggles into the gap.

"Well, it looks like Poison Ivy has made a home for herself," Batman observes as he looks out on the fantastic vista in front of him.

If Batman sees the park is now a swamp, turn to page 70.

If Batman discovers a giant vine castle, turn to page 89.

Batman decides that Harley will head for the fairgrounds. The circus is in town, and that's just the sort of place she feels at home. The Dark Knight spins the wheel of the Batmobile and speeds toward the Gotham City Fairgrounds.

It doesn't take long to reach his destination. When he arrives, the Dark Knight is just in time to hear a familiar sound.

FLAP! FLAP! FLAP!

"That's Harley's flat tire!" Batman realizes. He hears people screaming and yelling, too.

The Dark Knight fires a Batrope, and it anchors onto the Big Top's tentpole. Batman swings up to the peak. From this height he can see the entire fairgrounds. Sure enough, there's Harley's crazy little car swerving down the midway. She has picked up a driver.

"Catwoman!" Batman exclaims. "I don't know how she got back into the act, but I have to stop those two mischief makers before they hurt someone."

Turn the page.

The Dark Knight slides down the canopy of the circus Big Top. Before he reaches the end, he uses the canvas like a trampoline and bounces high into the air.

SPROINGGG! He sails through the air and onto the top of a smaller tent.

BOINGGG! The Dark Knight jumps and lands on his feet on the ground, right in front of Harley's car!

The feline felon swerves. She drives through a nearby tent without slowing down. The tent comes off its pegs and covers the vehicle like a giant sheet.

Batman follows the tire tracks on foot. He reaches a spot where the trail goes in two directions!

"How is that possible?" he wonders. All he knows is that he has to choose which set of tracks to follow.

If Batman pursues the trail to the left, turn to page 73.
If Batman follows the tracks to the right, turn to page 92.

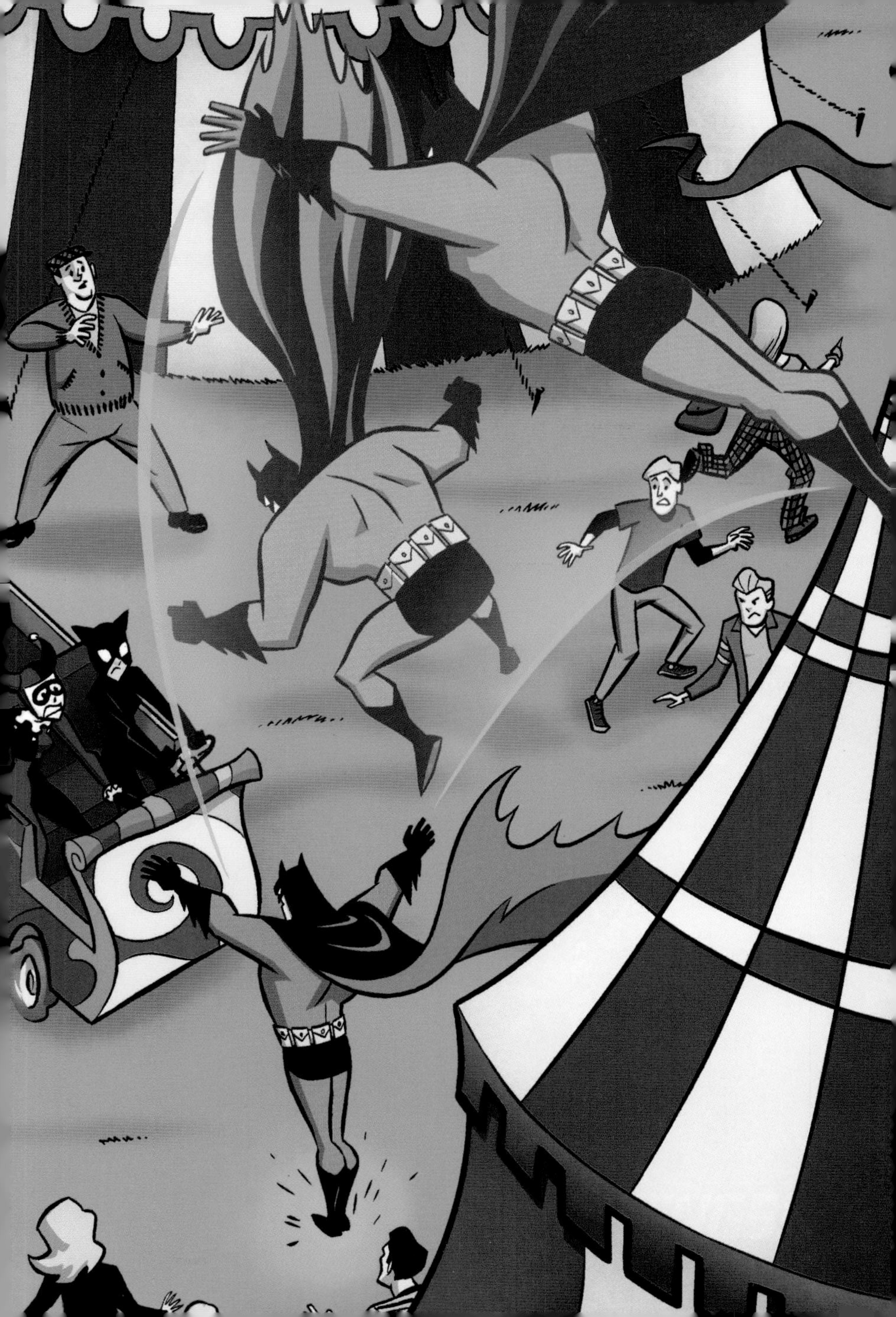

Batman leaps off the roof of the train and chases after Catwoman as she sprints toward the Champion Cat Show across the street. He is about to lasso her with a Batrope when she runs through the main door of the convention center.

The Dark Knight never slows down and follows her into the building.

A crowd of cat people suddenly surrounds the Caped Crusader! Cat owners and cat lovers pack the main hallway of the convention center. The crowd is dense and colorful, but Batman catches a glimpse of the dark-clad Catwoman not far away. She sees him, too, and runs!

Even though Catwoman flees her enemy, something sparkling catches her attention. A cat collar made of diamonds makes her pause.

"Ooh, *purr*-fection!" Catwoman sighs, snatching the priceless piece.

"Hey! Stop! Thief!" the jeweler yells.

Catwoman wraps the precious gems around her neck and scampers!

Batman pursues his feline foe into an exhibit hall of the convention center. The large room is a staging area for the kitty competitors and their human handlers. Hundreds of cats are being brushed, buffed, and blow-dried to make them look their best. But the felines are behaving badly. They meow and hiss and struggle in their helpers' hands.

Batman sees the reason why — Catwoman!

She stands on the far side of the hall and jiggles the diamond cat collar around her neck. The stones sparkle and create a hundred dots of light. Every cat in the place wants to chase the dots! Catwoman looks at Batman and smiles at her foe, knowing what she is about to unleash.

"Attack that big, bad, bat rat," Catwoman says as she directs the sparkling spots of light at Batman.

Turn to page 38.

Batman takes a flashlight from his Utility Belt and spots a trail of footprints leading to the left. Poison Ivy went this way!

The Dark Knight hurries down the drainage pipe in pursuit. The flashlight illuminates only a short distance ahead. The darkness and silence is spooky, but Batman isn't afraid. There isn't much that can surprise him. Except . . .

Batman halts when he comes to a forest of giant mushrooms growing in the drainage pipe. They are as tall as he is and reach to the top of the tunnel. The plants are growing so close together that they block Batman's path.

"Ivy is trying to keep me from following her," the Dark Knight concludes.

He takes a mini-laser from his Utility Belt and slices through the trunk of a mushroom tree. The giant fungus falls to one side with a soft plop.

Batman slowly works his way through the mushroom forest. He recognizes this species of fungus. It's harmless.

Even though the Dark Knight knows these plants aren't dangerous, he doesn't let down his guard. There's no telling what's ahead of him.

He finds out soon enough! Batman enters the heart of the mushroom forest. The plants here are extremely tall.

"I must be in one of the underground water tanks," Batman realizes. "It's a good thing it's empty right now."

The Dark Knight pushes past the last few stalks and sees his enemy resting on a soft cushion of glowing flowers and vines. The sweet scent of night-blooming jasmine floats through the air.

"Welcome to my underground arbor, Batman," Ivy says. "Every plant here thrives in the dark."

"So do I," Batman reminds her.

Turn to page 42.

Batman sees that the dinner cruiser is too far out in the water for Harley to have jumped aboard. The Dark Knight concludes that she is escaping through the shopping arcade. His theory is confirmed when he hears tourists yelling for help.

Batman races into the open-air mall and sees Harley stumbling and tripping over the members of a musical band. The drum set is booming, and the cymbals are crashing loudly. One of the musicians is swinging a tambourine at Harley.

TISSSH! TISSSH! The instrument makes a nice sound but annoys the Mistress of Mayhem.

"Stop it! That hurts my ears," Harley complains. She grabs the tambourine and tosses it into the air.

Batman catches the instrument and throws it back toward Harley. His aim is perfect. The tambourine drops down over her head and onto her shoulders.

DING-A-DING-DING! The noise makes Harley's ears ring! Her eyes roll in their sockets.

Harley halts in her tracks, and her spine straightens like a rod. Her whole body vibrates like a tuning fork!

Batman is about to put Bat-cuffs on the costumed culprit when one of the musicians snatches the tambourine off Harley's neck.

"Hey, that's mine!" the band member declares.

Suddenly, Harley recovers from the ringing in her ears. She sees the Dark Knight is about to capture her! She shoves the musician toward an open drainage grate under repair.

"Gotta run, Bats!" Harley laughs as the Dark Knight races to the rescue.

The Dark Knight stops the musician from falling into the hole. When he looks up, Harley is nowhere to be seen.

But he can *hear* where she is!

Turn to page 45.

The Dark Knight has faced many dangerous situations in his career, but he's never had to battle an army of champion show cats! He watches the horde of Persian, Siamese, Manx, and Maine coons rush toward him in a giant wave of felines.

"It's a good thing that bats can fly," Batman says as he fires a grapnel toward the ceiling.

Catwoman watches her foe rise into the air and escape the furry assault. She grumbles and runs through a nearby doorway. A hundred cats follow the sparkling cat collar she wears.

"Well, she'll be easy to track," Batman says.

The Dark Knight swings through the door and into the next room. It's the main showroom of the convention center. Catwoman stands in the middle of the hall surrounded by so many cats that she can't move. She's trapped!

Batman fires a grapnel into the ceiling rafters and swings toward Catwoman. He scoops her up into the air and lands on a catwalk above the confused kitties.

"Let's end this game of cat and mouse," Batman suggests.

"I'm the cat, so that makes you the mouse," Catwoman replies.

"I thought you called me a big, bad, bat rat," the Dark Knight reminds her.

"Oh, did I hurt your feelings? What are a few friendly insults between archenemies?" Catwoman grins.

As quick as a cat, she snatches the Batrope out of the Dark Knight's grasp. She swings over to another lofty catwalk and runs along it to a ladder leading back down to the showroom floor.

Batman sprints to the end of the walkway he's on and starts to climb down, too. He looks over at the fleeing felon and sees her squirming into an air conditioning vent.

The Dark Knight takes a small computer tablet from his Utility Belt and calls up a map of the ventilation system. He traces the ductwork and finds where Catwoman will exit.

Turn the page.

Batman slides down the rest of the ladder and races to a room with a display of Famous Felines of History. He spots a giant statue of the Egyptian cat goddess, Bast, and hides behind it.

Catwoman pops out of the airshaft moments later, smiling to herself. That smile vanishes as soon as a Batrope wraps around her body.

She struggles to claw her way to freedom, but Batman tightens the Batrope like a leash.

"Surrender like a good kitty, and I'll give you a nice, big bowl of ice cream," the Dark Knight suggests.

"Well, why didn't you say that earlier?" Catwoman says, yielding to the Batman.

THE END

To follow another path, turn to page 11.

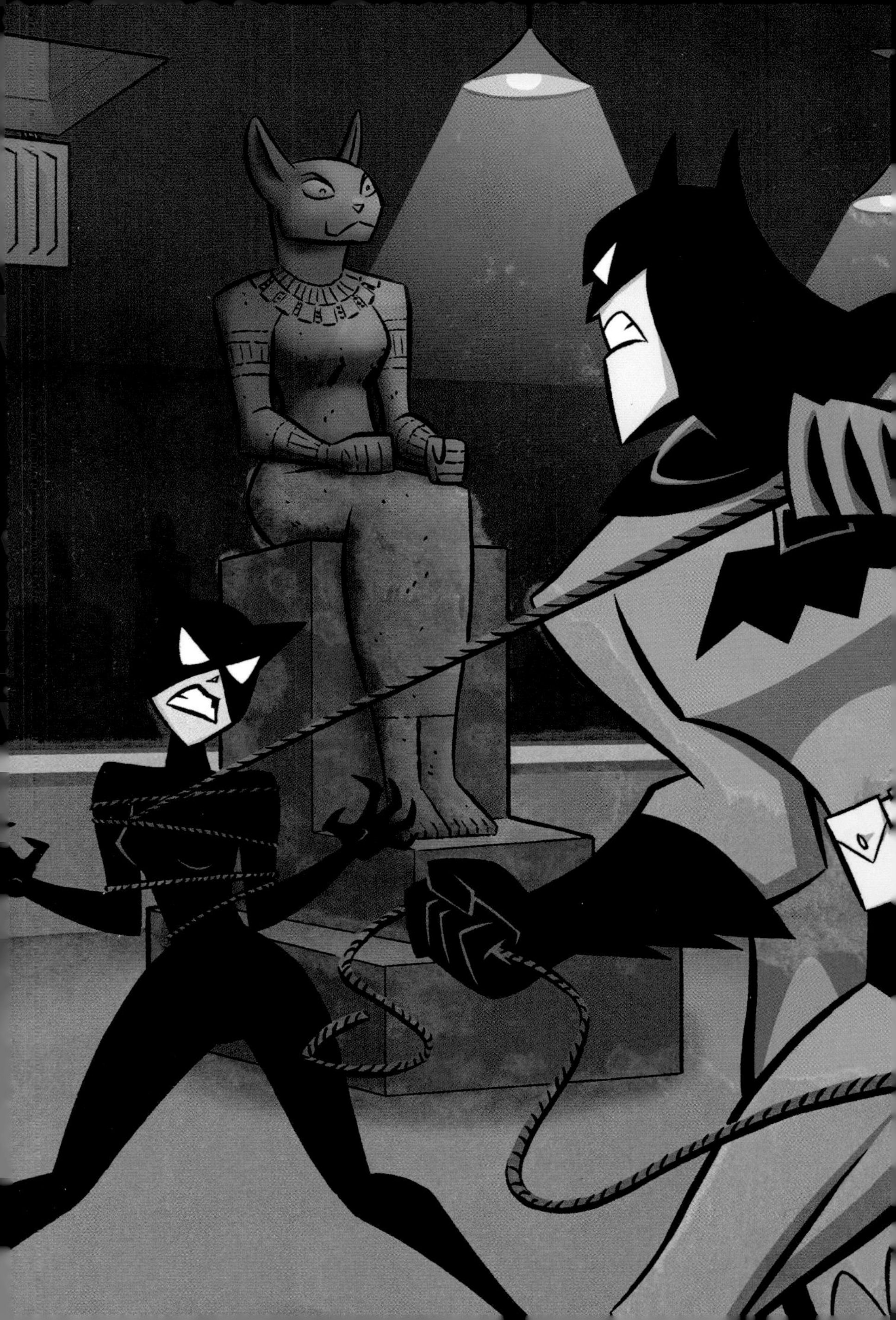

Poison Ivy gestures with one hand, and a giant night lily stretches out toward the Batman. Its pale white petals open and close like the jaws of a hungry shark. Batman leaps out of the way and throws a sharp Batarang at the stem.

SNIIIIK! The flower head is cut from the stem. Both wither at once.

"It looks like I have a black thumb," the Dark Knight observes.

"Don't worry. I have an excellent green thumb," Ivy replies.

Poison Ivy commands several moonflower vines to rise up and curl around Batman. Before they can trap him completely, the Dark Knight cuts through them with the sharp points of the Batarang. Suddenly, his nose is assaulted by an awful smell! The damaged plants start to stink.

"Phew! What is that? Rotten peanut butter?" Batman coughs and covers his nose and mouth.

"See? My plants can fight you in different ways," Ivy explains.

Batman grabs one of the smelly vines and uses it to swing over to Poison Ivy.

"Yes, your plants *do* have many uses," the Dark Knight observes.

Ivy frowns and commands the sticky stems of some night-flowering catchfly plants to grow up around the Dark Knight. The moment they touch him, Batman is caught like an insect on the strands of a spiderweb.

He struggles to get free as Ivy strolls over to him. A kiss forms on her lips. Batman realizes she is about to blow a gust of her mind-control spore-breath on him.

The Dark Knight knows there is only one thing he can do. He lunges forward and rams Ivy with his shoulder like a football player. She gasps as she falls backward. She is forced to inhale instead of exhale. This gives Batman the chance to break free from the sticky plant stems.

The Dark Knight fires a grapnel upward. Its speed and weight bursts open a manhole cover above his head.

Turn the page.

The red and blue lights of police vehicles flash and bounce inside the underground arbor. Poison Ivy shuts her eyes against the glare.

Batman uses this to his advantage. He grabs her and wraps his arms around her. She can't get loose! She's stuck to the goo the catchfly plant has left on his costume.

"It's time to uproot this Ivy," the Dark Knight declares.

Batman and his captive rise up out of the dark underground and into the lights of a large police force.

"Phew! What's that smell?" Commissioner Gordon asks as he unsticks Poison Ivy from the Dark Knight.

"That would be me," Batman admits. "You know, sometime my job really stinks."

THE END

To follow another path, turn to page 11.

Batman follows the sounds of destruction. He runs into the Arts and Crafts Plaza. It looks as if a whirlwind hit it.

Whirlwind Harley!

Handmade sculptures are broken and scattered. Original paintings are torn and splattered. A stand with homemade cookies is crushed.

As the people pick up the pieces, Batman picks up a clue. He notices a trail of cookie crumbs going down the boardwalk. It leads him to a small park section of the seaport. That's where he sees the Mistress of Menace sitting on a park bench, stuffing a handful of stolen cookies into her mouth. She sees him, too.

"Rou ran't ratch re!" Harley declares through a mouth stuffed full of cookies.

"I can catch you, and I will," Batman replies. "By the way, didn't anyone tell you it's rude to talk with your mouth full?"

Harley doesn't answer. She runs!

Turn the page.

Batman follows her to an exhibit of Tall Ship sailing vessels. There is a display of full-size ships anchored at the Seaport as an attraction for tourists. Harley runs up one of the gangplanks.

"Avast, me hearties!" Harley shouts as she scampers up a rope ladder and into the rigging.

Batman watches her climb up the main mast of the square-rigged ship. He fires a Batrope onto one of the yardarms and zips upward. The Dark Knight meets Harley high above the deck.

"Heave to and surrender, Harley," Batman orders.

"I won't take a broadside from the dread Captain Batman!" Harley retorts. She runs along the spar, shouting to an imaginary crew. "Hoist the anchor! Lower the mainsail! Full speed ahead!"

Harley leaps off the spar! Batman is about to throw a Batrope and catch her, but she grabs onto the mainstay line and slides along it toward the deck.

"So I'm the dread Captain Batman, eh? Okay, I can play along," the Dark Knight decides.

Batman swoops down on the Batrope like a pirate and scoops up Harley as soon as her feet touch the deck.

"Arrr!" the Dark Knight growls. "You're . . . er . . . yer me captive now!"

"Oh! I surrender to the scourge of the seven seas!" Harley sighs. "How romantic!"

Police race up the gangplank and surround the duo. Batman hands Harley over to the authorities.

"My crew will take you to your cabin now," the Dark Knight tells the misguided miss. "A nice, safe cell in Arkham."

THE END

To follow another path, turn to page 11.

Batman watches Catwoman leap from the roof of the train and land in the passenger seat of an open car. The vehicle looks like a car from a roller coaster. The driver is Harley Quinn!

"She must have followed the train," Batman concludes as he swings down to the street.

Catwoman waves goodbye at Batman as Harley laughs madly and steps on the gas. The Dark Knight quickly takes a miniature dart launcher from his Utility Belt and fires a tracking chip toward the fleeing vehicle.

KA-CLINK!

The device attaches to the bumper. Batman pulls out a small receiver and watches a bright blinking dot travel along a map of Gotham City.

"They've got a head start, but I can still catch up to them," Batman says.

The super hero pulls a wireless microphone from his Utility Belt and speaks into it. "Voice command, activate. Acquire my location beacon and hone in."

A few minutes later, a one-man Bat-Copter flies toward the Dark Knight. He watches it land on autopilot in the middle of the empty nighttime street.

Batman jumps into the open-air pilot's seat and takes off again into the night sky. He guides the craft high above the streets of Gotham City, using the tracking device to trail Harley and Catwoman. He hardly needs it to find them.

The shrill sounds of car horns and yelling pedestrians lead Batman to the sight of Harley driving through the late-night traffic like a madwoman. She doesn't always stay on the street.

"Yaaaa haaaa!" Harley Quinn howls. She's having fun weaving in and out of traffic.

"Yaaaa!" Catwoman yells. She isn't enjoying the joyride.

Flying above them in the Bat-Copter, the Caped Crusader can see something ahead that they can't. Their car is speeding toward a drawbridge that is raised in the up position.

Turn the page.

Harley heads straight toward the hazard as if she's unaware of it. Batman flies the Bat-Copter alongside the car and waves at Harley.

"Stop! Get over!" the Dark Knight shouts, making wide motions with his arms.

"Go away, you buzzing bat!" Harley replies.

The Mistress of Mayhem turns her attention to Batman and takes her eyes off the road. She swerves wildly.

SCREEEECH! THUMP! The car bounces up onto the curb and barely misses a streetlight, but at least it misses going over the drawbridge.

"Take the wheel!" Harley tells Catwoman, abandoning the driver's seat.

"What are you doing?!" Catwoman yelps, lunging to grab control of the car.

Harley Quinn scrambles into the backseat of the vehicle and lifts the cushion. She pulls what looks like a squirt-gun cannon from a hidden storage space. Batman knows that looks are deceiving when it comes to Harley Quinn!

Turn to page 58.

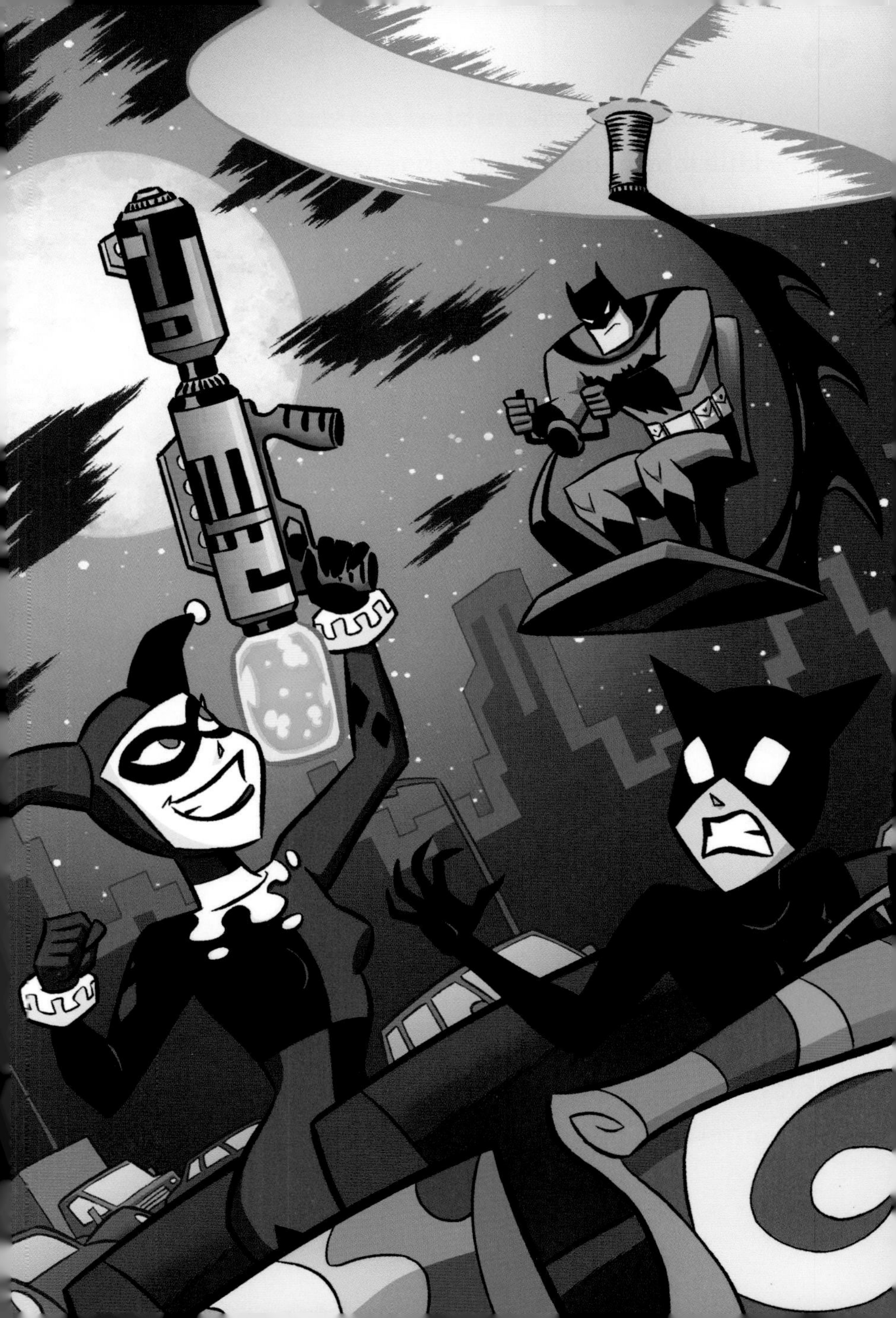

The Dark Knight spots a faint clue in the darkness of the drainage pipe. He sees flower petals floating in the water. Poison Ivy has gone down the right-hand branch of the T-junction!

"She must have sprouted some random seeds in the water without knowing it," Batman deduces.

The tunnel stretches away into the darkness, but the super hero can see a dim glow in the distance.

"Poison Ivy will head for the light just like a plant," the Caped Crusader realizes. He runs toward it, too.

Batman reaches the source of the light and is startled to see a huge hole torn in the pipe made by giant, thorny roses. The twisted stems look like living barbed wire.

The Dark Knight can hear people yelling on the other side of the opening. They sound alarmed and very afraid! He rushes through the opening to help!

Batman sees that he is in a laboratory. There are giant vats of bubbling liquids and rows and rows of vegetables. At first glance Batman can identify zucchini, yellow summer squash, and green beans.

Lab workers run around, shouting and trying to escape mammoth pumpkin vines swarming all over the room. One of the tendrils has several scientists in its grip.

The Dark Knight leaps to the rescue! He takes a capsule from his Utility Belt and smashes it against the side of the mutant vine. Ice spreads out along the whole length of the plant.

SSMAAAASH! Batman cracks the frozen vine and frees the captives.

Other workers are still in danger. Batman looks around the lab for a solution and finds it in the form of a big red button on the wall: **FIRE SUPPRESSION**. The Dark Knight sees that it's made by Wayne Enterprises. He knows exactly what it can do.

Batman pushes the big red button on the wall.

Turn the page.

WHHOOOOSH! Thick fog sprays out of the lab ceiling. Suddenly all the plants start to wilt! The human workers are not harmed. They run from the room to safety while Batman searches for Poison Ivy.

"Surrender, Ivy!" he demands loudly.

"Oh! Don't hurt me!" a female voice replies.

The Dark Knight sees a woman in a white lab coat holding a potted plant. She stands shaking in her lab shoes in front of the emergency exit.

"Who are you?" Batman asks.

"I . . . I'm Ivy. I'm a scientist here. You . . . you said to surrender," the woman stammers. "I just wanted to save my favorite plant from the fire suppression chemicals."

"Sorry, wrong Ivy," the Dark Knight says.

A moment later, Batman spots another woman in a white lab coat. He is suspicious, but hesitates. She could be just another innocent lab worker.

"Wait, her shoes are wrong," Batman notices.

Turn to page 62.

The Dark Knight spots Harley in the control room on the bridge of the dinner-cruise ship as it pulls away from the pier.

SPLAAASSH! She throws the captain and his first officer over the side and into the water. The Mistress of Mayhem has hijacked the boat!

"It's too far to jump, even for me," Batman realizes as he judges the distance between him and the vessel. "And the angle is wrong to swing with a Batrope."

The Dark Knight turns and runs back down the boardwalk. Harley watches and thinks he is running away.

"Hahaha! Batman is a chicken!" she laughs.

The Dark Knight isn't running away. He's running toward the Batboat tied up at the end of the pier. He jumps in and throws the throttle forward.

VROOOOMMM! The engines roar to life.

"Stealth mode," Batman gives the voice command.

Turn the page.

Holographic panels on the hull shimmer. The speedboat looks just like the surface of the water.

The boat seems to disappear!

The loud engines quiet to a murmur. They have just as much power and speed but now are as silent as a whisper. Certain that he is pretty much invisible, the Dark Knight navigates the Batboat toward the stern of the cruiser. It takes less than a minute to reach the hijacked vessel.

Batman ties onto the cruiser and jumps aboard. None of the dinner guests in the restaurant notice the Dark Knight climb up to the top deck. He works his way to the ship's bridge. A screeching sound makes him pause.

"Yo, ho, blow the bat down!" Harley Quinn sings at the top of her voice. *"Tickle my timbers and show the guy home, roll on the floor and blow the man down!"*

The Dark Knight is sure that none of the song lyrics are correct, but at least Harley has her guard down. He takes a pair of Bat-cuffs from his Utility Belt and enters the bridge.

"Save the poor sailor, any port in a storm, hi, ho, man overboard!" Harley howls off-key.

"Your singing is a crime all by itself," the Dark Knight declares. He tosses a Batrope at the sour singer.

Harley dodges the lasso and drops to the deck. She rolls like the sailor in her crazy song.

"Abandon ship!" Harley yells as she jumps out of the window.

Turn to page 65.

Batman faces the squirting end of a water cannon in the hands of Harley Quinn. He knows he has to expect the unexpected from the Mistress of Mayhem. Sure enough! **SQUIIIIIDGE!** A stream of purple liquid shoots out from the goofy gun.

The Dark Knight veers the Bat-Copter away just in time. The liquid turns to goo when it comes in contact with the cool night air. The goop strikes the side of a building and sticks to it like a big blob of chewing gum!

"That's going to leave a mess, but it gives me an idea," Batman observes.

The Caped Crusader accelerates the Bat-Copter and flies ahead of the kooky roller-coaster car. He pilots the copter backward in front of the vehicle and waves at Catwoman and Harley.

"What is he up to?" Catwoman wonders.

"Who cares!" Harley shrieks, firing the goo gun at her enemy.

The purple liquid shoots at the Bat-Copter.

SPLUUUUDGE! It misses the aircraft as the Dark Knight swerves out of the way. The goop splashes onto the road in front of Harley's car.

"Uh-oh," Catwoman gulps as she suddenly realizes what Batman is up to.

The cool wind from the Bat-Copter's helicopter blades hits the purple liquid, and it starts to transform into goo. Catwoman can't avoid driving over the sticky stuff. The tires get stuck, and the car comes to a sudden stop.

Harley somersaults through the air from the backseat and lands safely on her feet. A dozen squirt cannons get tossed from the storage seat and scatter all around her. Catwoman grips the steering wheel as a clown-face airbag deploys.

Harley reaches for the nearest goo gun. ***SMAAAACK!*** A Batarang knocks it out of her hand. She looks up and sees the Dark Knight hovering in the Bat-Copter.

BANG! Batman and Harley see Catwoman standing in the driver's seat of the roller-coaster car. The clown-face air bag is in shreds.

Turn the page.

Catwoman's claws are the cause of its explosive destruction. Batman watches from the Bat-Copter as Catwoman jumps out of the car and marches over to Harley Quinn.

"Kid, you are *crazy!*" Catwoman declares.

"Gee, thanks!" Harley smiles.

"She's all yours! I'm going home to eat a pint of ice cream," Catwoman tells Batman as she waves her hands in the air and leaves.

"What? Hey!" Harley protests.

The Dark Knight snags Harley with a net and hooks it to the side of the copter. He flies after Catwoman.

"You're overloaded and off balance," Catwoman observes. Then she laughs. "You don't have to let me go, but I bet you can't catch me!"

Catwoman starts to run. Batman follows. He knows the game of cat and mouse will never end.

THE END

To follow another path, turn to page 11.

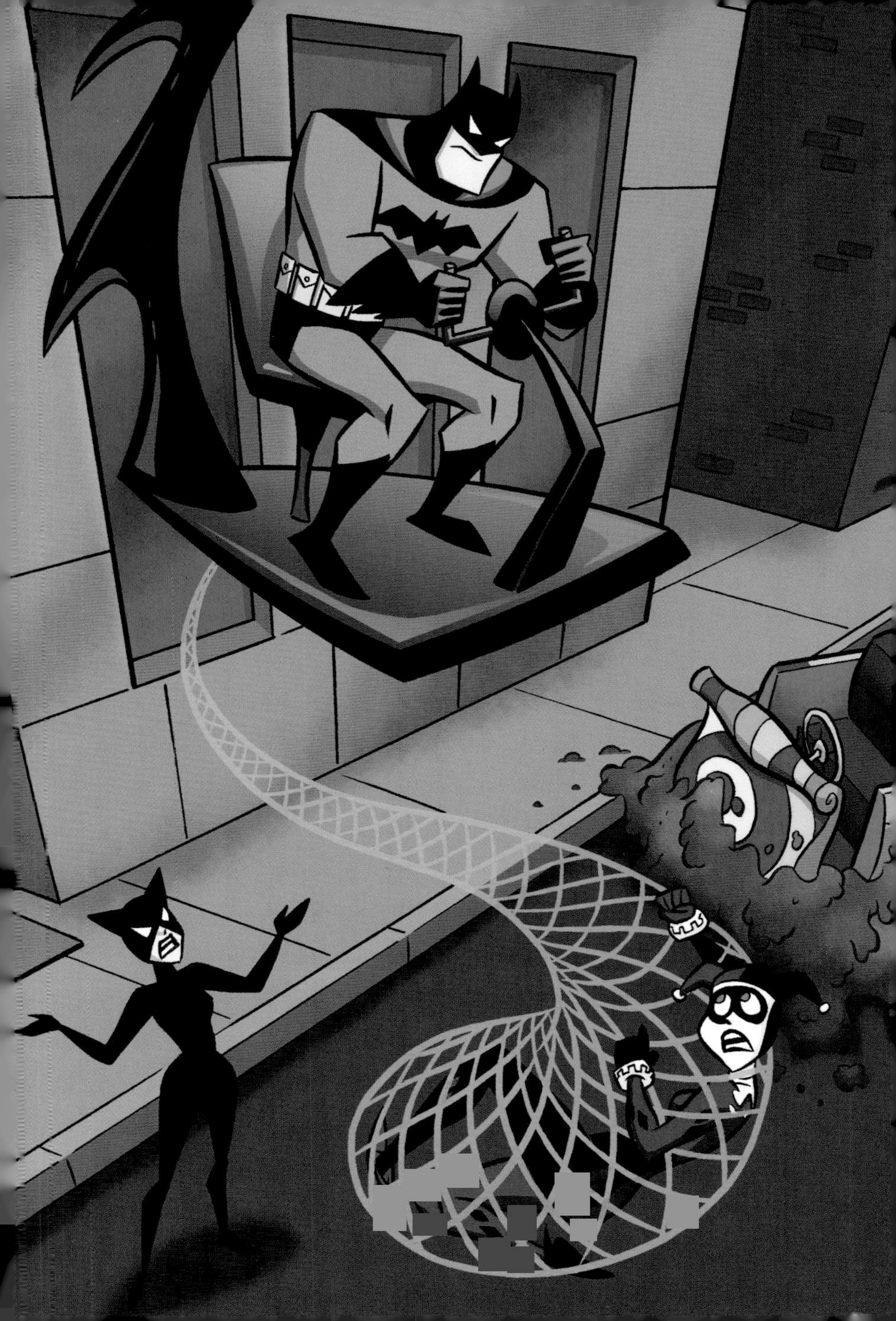

Batman sees that the suspicious woman isn't wearing lab shoes. Her footwear belongs to . . .

"Poison Ivy!" Batman shouts.

The Dark Knight races after his foe. She runs away, and he notices that she doesn't send a single vine or poisonous plant to attack him.

Ivy doesn't dare let Batman know that the chemicals have weakened her. She is immune to almost every toxin, but there is something in the fire-fighting fog that has weakened her. Right now her power over plants is not very strong.

"But I still have some power over people," Ivy says.

Ivy blends in with a group of fleeing lab workers. She exhales her mind-control spores into the crowd, and the people are mindless drones ready to obey her every command.

"Get Batman!" Poison Ivy instructs her new slaves.

The workers turn away from escape and toward the Dark Knight instead.

Batman faces the hypnotized horde. He holds a Batarang in his hand but hesitates to use it. He doesn't want to hurt anyone. They are innocent civilians, and they don't know what they're doing.

One of the scientists tries to punch the Dark Knight. The man swings his fist and misses.

A lab worker tries to grab Batman but trips and falls down. *THUUUMP!* The Caped Crusader soon discovers that it's very easy to avoid getting hit by any of the workers. They are not trained fighters like he is. No one has any experience.

Batman makes his way through Ivy's army with no trouble. He doesn't have to defend himself very hard. All he needs to do is give a person a gentle shove now and then whenever someone tries to attack him. He walks through the clumsy crowd and finally comes face-to-face with his primary foe, Poison Ivy!

The Dark Knight tightens his grip around the Batarang in his hand. He is ready to throw it and wrap up the Princess of Plants with the Batrope attached to it.

Turn the page.

"Wait. I need your help," Ivy whispers. Her voice is weak. Her body seems frail. She isn't a fearsome super-villainess anymore.

Batman folds up the Batarang and Batrope and puts them back into his Utility Belt.

"Of course I'll help you. Release the lab workers from your mind-control spores," the Dark Knight says.

"Done," Ivy agrees.

The crowd wakes up and heads for the exits as Batman snaps Bat-cuffs on his foe.

"The fire suppression fog . . . did something to me . . ." Ivy says.

In his other identity as Bruce Wayne, Batman knows all about the fire suppressant made by Wayne Enterprises.

"I know," the Dark Knight reveals. "I triggered it on purpose to stop you. You can recover at Arkham."

THE END

To follow another path, turn to page 11.

Harley Quinn makes a fast exit from the bridge of the dinner-cruise boat. Batman is right behind her as she runs along the roof of the restaurant section. The crazy criminal crashes down through a skylight hatch and lands in the middle of the dining area.

SMAAAASH! Batman lands right next to her. The dinner guests shriek in shock.

"Red alert! Negative control at helm!" Harley announces wildly.

She grabs a handful of tomatoes from the salad bar and throws them at the Caped Crusader. *THWAAP! THWAAAP!* He knocks them aside with the backs of his hands.

Suddenly, large vines grow up out of a smashed tomato. The seeds sprout and wrap around the Dark Knight.

"Poison Ivy!" Batman gasps as the tendrils tighten.

"Ivy! I'm so glad you're here!" Harley cheers.

"We're partners in crime, after all," Ivy replies.

Turn the page.

The Queen of Green strides up to Batman as he struggles to break free of the vines. She puckers her lips to blow her mind-control spores at the Dark Knight. If he inhales them, he will be her mind slave. There's no way for him to reach his Utility Belt for a filter mask!

SPLOOOSH! A ripe tomato smacks the Caped Crusader in the face.

"Haha! I got him!" Harley celebrates. She dances a victory dance.

"Thanks, that's just what I needed. The tomato pulp protected me from Ivy's spores," Batman reveals as he slices free from the vines with a sharp Batarang.

"Uh-oh," Harley and Ivy gulp.

The Dark Knight throws a net toward the two. Ivy knocks it aside with the fronds of a potted fern. Harley jumps onto a dining table and throws some knives and forks at her enemy. Batman dodges out of the way. The cutlery hits the plants instead.

"Harley! You're hurting my plants!" Ivy yells.

"Oops! Sorry!" Harley says. "Batman made me do it!"

"It's time to leave," Ivy announces.

The Queen of Green commands a nearby plant to wrap around her and Harley. It lifts them up through the restaurant skylight hatch and into the open air.

WHUUUP! WHUUUP! WHEE-OOOH! A fleet of police boats and helicopters are there to meet the villains. Spotlights focus on the two criminals.

"Where's a white flag when you need one?" Harley groans.

"Bat-cuffs work," the Dark Knight says as he takes the two felons into custody.

THE END

To follow another path, turn to page 11.

Batman deduces that Catwoman and Poison Ivy will go to the Botanical Gardens. It's home turf for Ivy. She can control the thousands of plants there. The Dark Knight knows he has to get to the Gardens before them — and fast.

There is no more traffic on the road at this hour. Batman can't hitch a ride like the female felons did. He has to find another way.

WHUPPP! WHUPPP! The Dark Knight hears the sound of a helicopter. He looks up and sees a news chopper.

"They must be covering the robbery at the charity event," Batman concludes. "They are about to be a part of the story."

The Dark Knight uses a grapnel to snag a landing strut on the helicopter. He swoops up onto the strut. ***TAP! TAP! TAP!*** Batman raps on the cockpit door.

"Whaaa?" the pilot shouts in surprise.

"I'm in pursuit of two criminals and need to get to the Botanical Gardens," Batman reveals.

"I can take you wherever you want to go," the pilot offers. "I'm a retired police officer and glad to help."

"Thank you," Batman says.

"Hold on," the pilot warns as he accelerates the aircraft.

"Wow! Now this is what I call news!" the reporter says from the backseat.

The Dark Knight rides outside on the helicopter strut as it flies over Gotham City. It doesn't take long to reach their destination. Batman sees the city bus pulling to a stop just outside the main gate of the Botanical Gardens. He watches Catwoman and Poison Ivy jump down from the roof of the vehicle.

"There they are," Batman says to the pilot, pointing to the two costumed criminals.

Turn to page 75.

Poison Ivy has turned Gotham Park into a swampland. The grass and sidewalks are under water. Strings of Spanish moss hang from the tree branches, and giant cattail reeds stand in giant clumps.

"It looks like a bayou in here," Batman says.

The Dark Knight can see Ivy's giant green carpet floating not far away. The living platform is high and dry in the middle of the soggy surroundings. Harley's car is not so lucky.

BLUUUB! BLUUUB! It's sinking into the muck. The Mistress of Merry sits on the floating carpet. She isn't laughing. She looks wet and unhappy.

"Cheer up!" Ivy tells her partner in crime. "Batman can't get us in here."

The Dark Knight knows she's wrong about that! He looks around for a way to get to the floating platform.

Suddenly, he sees something moving in the water. It's an alligator, but it's made of twisted vines and has giant thorns for teeth!

Turn to page 72.

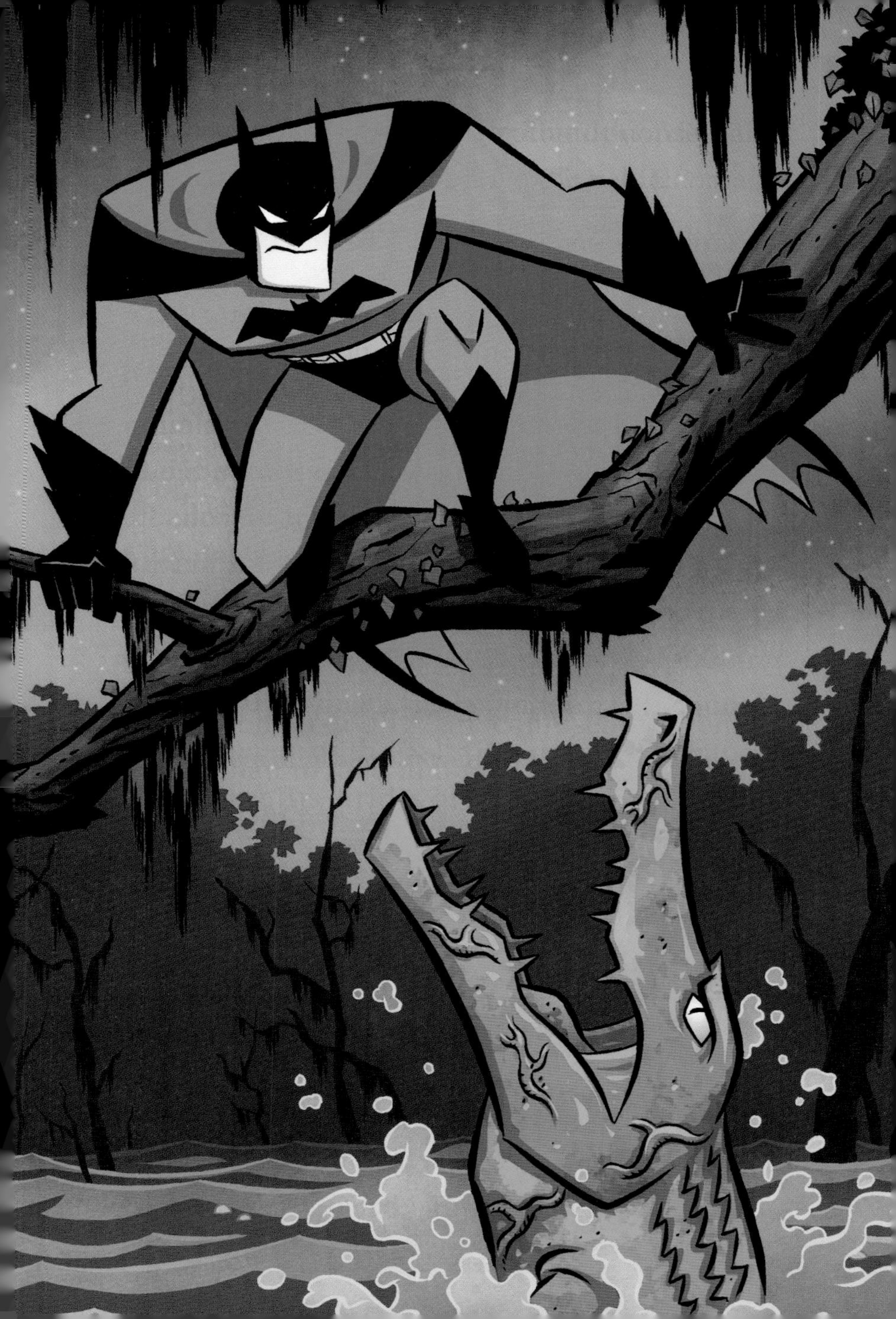

Batman knows he has to get to the platform and rescue the party guest being held hostage. The plant gator guards the water below, so the Dark Knight decides to climb higher into the trees. He works his way along the woven branches.

The thick, hanging moss hides Batman from view. Ivy and Harley don't see him slowly making his way toward the green platform. But the moss hides something from Batman, too. A vine the size of a boa constrictor slowly slides down from a branch above his head. It slithers through the hanging moss toward the Dark Knight.

It brings friends.

Turn to page 79.

The Dark Knight decides to trace the tire tracks to the left. As he runs along the midway he hears screaming, but that could be people having fun on the rides. Suddenly he is almost trampled by a fleeing crowd. Batman runs against the tide and sees Harley's roller-coaster car stuck on the merry-go-round.

The carousel is spinning very fast. Batman sees why. Harley Quinn is at the controls! The people on the ride are trapped on the not-so-merry-go-round.

"Oooh, everything's still spinning," Catwoman moans. She stands nearby and wobbles.

Batman takes advantage of her dizziness and tosses a Batarang. A net pops out and drops down over the feline felon. It doesn't stay on her for long.

"Reowr!" Catwoman hisses, shredding the net with her sharp claws. "I might be dizzy, but I'm not defenseless."

Catwoman lunges at the Dark Knight with her claws.

Turn the page.

Batman avoids her attack and is ready for more, but he hears people yelling for help. There are riders still trapped on the carousel. He has to save them first. His battle with Catwoman will have to wait.

The Dark Knight jumps onto the merry-go-round and makes his way toward the control booth at the core. It's the only part of the ride that isn't revolving. He catches glimpses of Harley at the controls as he goes around and around. She sees him, too. Once, twice, three times, then suddenly he is in the doorway.

"Wait your turn! I'm driving this thing!" Harley declares.

She yanks on the speed lever, and it breaks off in her hand. She grins at Batman's shocked expression.

"Oops!" Harley laughs.

Turn to page 82.

The ex-police pilot drops the news helicopter toward Catwoman and Poison Ivy. They look up at the sound of the rotor engines and see a remarkable sight! The Dark Knight descends out of the night sky gripping the side of a chopper and heads straight for them like a black hawk.

"He just doesn't give up!" Catwoman gasps.

"Get to the greenhouse!" Ivy shouts to her partner in crime.

Poison Ivy plants her feet and raises her arms. A nearby grove of trees begins to grow at a stupendous rate. The leafy branches extend toward the helicopter like grasping hands.

"Evasive maneuvers!" the pilot yells, pulling back on the control stick. The copter ascends to avoid the danger.

Batman grips the landing strut as the chopper banks away, but he doesn't take his gaze off of the felons. He sees them enter the greenhouse.

"I need to get on the ground. Now!" Batman tells the pilot.

Turn the page.

"Affirmative," the man replies.

The helicopter lands on the paved plaza of the Botanical Gardens. Batman jumps off the landing strut and runs toward the greenhouse. He doesn't notice the news reporter getting out of the chopper to follow him.

The Dark Knight enters the greenhouse and faces a wall of thorny roses grown to stupendous size.

"I don't have time to stop and smell the roses," Batman says as he wraps his cape around him and pushes through the thick barrier.

There is a water garden on the other side. Catwoman reclines on a bed of cattail stalks, and Poison Ivy rests on a giant lily pad. They snack on strawberries the size of softballs.

"I could get used to this," Catwoman purrs happily.

"Me, too," Ivy declares. "I'm the Queen of Green, and this is going to be my palace. Look, here's my first loyal subject."

A giant lily blossom rises from the water and opens to reveal the news reporter! Batman sees this and leaps into action. He runs across the water plants like stepping-stones and grabs the reporter.

PWFFFT! Batman fires a Batrope and swings him to safety.

"Hands up! Everybody freeze!" a voice commands. Police officers swarm into the greenhouse. The helicopter pilot is with them.

Catwoman and Ivy freeze in surprise. The Dark Knight swoops down as silent as a bat and clamps the costumed criminals into Bat-cuffs.

"I called for backup," the pilot tells the Dark Knight.

"Batman! I need a picture of the hero!" the reporter says.

"Sure," Batman replies, turning the camera toward the helicopter pilot.

THE END

To follow another adventure, turn to page 11.

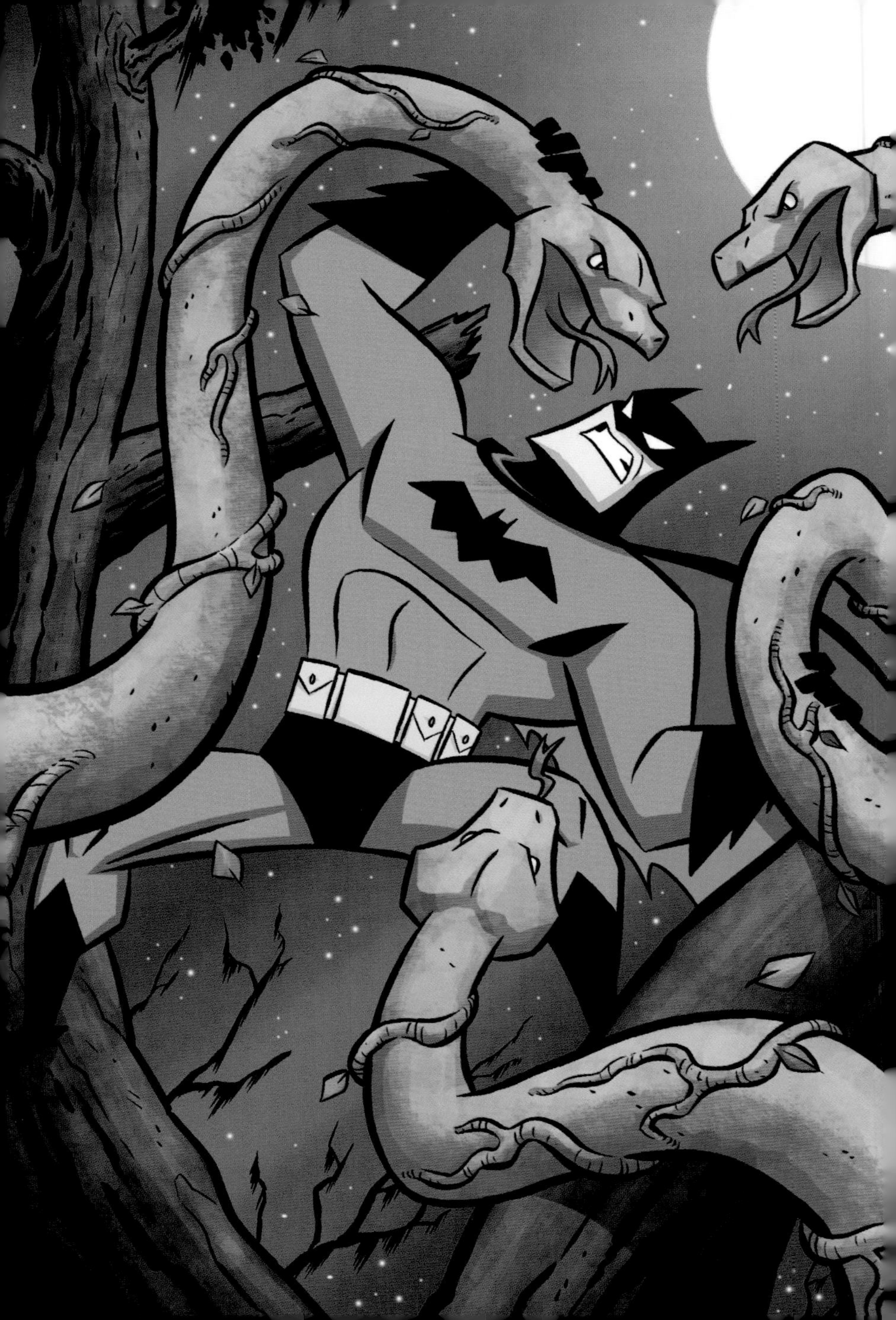

Batman's trained reflexes help him knock the snake vine away before it gets around his neck!

"I see Ivy set some traps," the Dark Knight observes.

A second later another vine slithers toward him. Then another. And another! A vine grabs one of his wrists. Two more tendrils wrap around his ankles. Suddenly there are too many for even the Caped Crusader to handle. He tries to pull free as hard as he can. The branches shake all around him.

"What's happening up there?" Harley wonders as she looks up at the shaking tree limbs.

"My vine guards must have caught an intruder," Ivy says. "It's probably Batman."

"You said he couldn't get us in here," Harley reminds her partner.

"He's like a weed. He always pops up," Poison Ivy sighs.

"Well, I'm going to bring him down," Harley vows.

Turn the page.

Harley grins as she aims a slingshot toward the trees. She fires a large marble into the branches. The tree limbs shatter, and something big drops into the swamp water. *SPLAAAASH!*

"Harley! Those are my plants!" Ivy protests.

"It's okay. I brought down Batman," Harley replies. "I think."

"Well, whoever it was, my plant gators will get him," Ivy declares.

Several of Ivy's vine constructs slither toward the spot of splashdown. Even though they are rooted in the swamp mud, they move quickly. Batman treads water and sees them coming toward him at eye level! He reaches into his Utility Belt. He tosses a capsule toward the creatures. It hits the water and releases a powder that withers the plant gators. They thrash wildly as they fall apart.

Ivy and Harley are too busy watching the splashing in the distance to notice the Dark Knight climbing onto the plant platform right behind them.

Batman slowly lifts himself out of the swamp. The tangled roots and vines of Poison Ivy's living green carpet are perfect handholds.

The Dark Knight is covered with dripping moss and weeds. He looks more like a swamp thing than a man!

He tosses a net over Ivy and Harley and catches them like a pair of bayou catfish. A quick squirt of some knockout spray from his Utility Belt puts the felons to sleep. As soon as Ivy starts to snooze, her control over the plant constructions is broken. The swamp water drains into the sewers, and the tree barrier unravels. An army of police rushes in as Batman helps the hostage out of the wilting flower prison.

"These costumed criminals sure leave a mess," Commissioner Gordon says.

"Look on the bright side. The city gardeners will have mulch and compost for months," Batman replies.

THE END

To follow another path, turn to page 11.

Harley looks at the broken speed lever in her hand and then at Batman. She laughs like a hyena.

"Okay, you can drive now!" Harley says as she throws the lever at the Dark Knight.

Batman catches the lever in one hand. He pulls a set of Bat-cuffs from his Utility Belt with his other hand. Harley backs up against the wall. There is nowhere for her to flee. The Dark Knight is between her and the door.

Suddenly, he is tackled from behind. Sharp claws shred his cape.

"Catwoman!" Batman realizes.

Harley scampers past the Dark Knight as he battles Catwoman. As soon as her partner is free, Catwoman flees, too. Batman lets them go. For now. He has to stop the merry-go-round!

The Dark Knight disconnects the electrical wires on the control panel. The carousel slows down and finally stops. The riders are very dizzy, but they are safe.

"Harley and Catwoman got away, but they can't have gotten too far on foot," Batman says. "Their car is still stuck in the merry-go-round."

The super hero hears cries for help. The partners in crime haven't gone far, and already they are causing trouble!

Batman follows the sounds of confusion and finds Harley stealing stuffed toys from a game booth. Catwoman sits on a pile of plush toy kitty cats and eats from a big tub of ice cream.

Batman launches a Batrope and snags the top of the Test Your Strength pole. He uses it to swing toward the villain. She sees him coming but can't move. Her tummy is full of ice cream.

"Buuuurp! Uh-oh," Catwoman says.

This time when the Dark Knight nets Catwoman she's too tired to fight. She curls up in her pillowy pile and takes a catnap.

Harley looks at Catwoman and then at Batman. She drops the stuffed toys and holds out her wrists in surrender.

Turn the page.

"This isn't fun anymore," she whimpers and starts to cry.

Batman snaps Bat-cuffs on Harley. As police surround the partners in crime, Batman gives Harley an ice cream cone. She looks up at him and sniffs back her tears.

"You're a good guy . . . for an archenemy," Harley says.

The Dark Knight puts a finger up to his lips.

"Shhh. I won't tell if you won't," Batman replies.

THE END

To follow another path, turn to page 11.

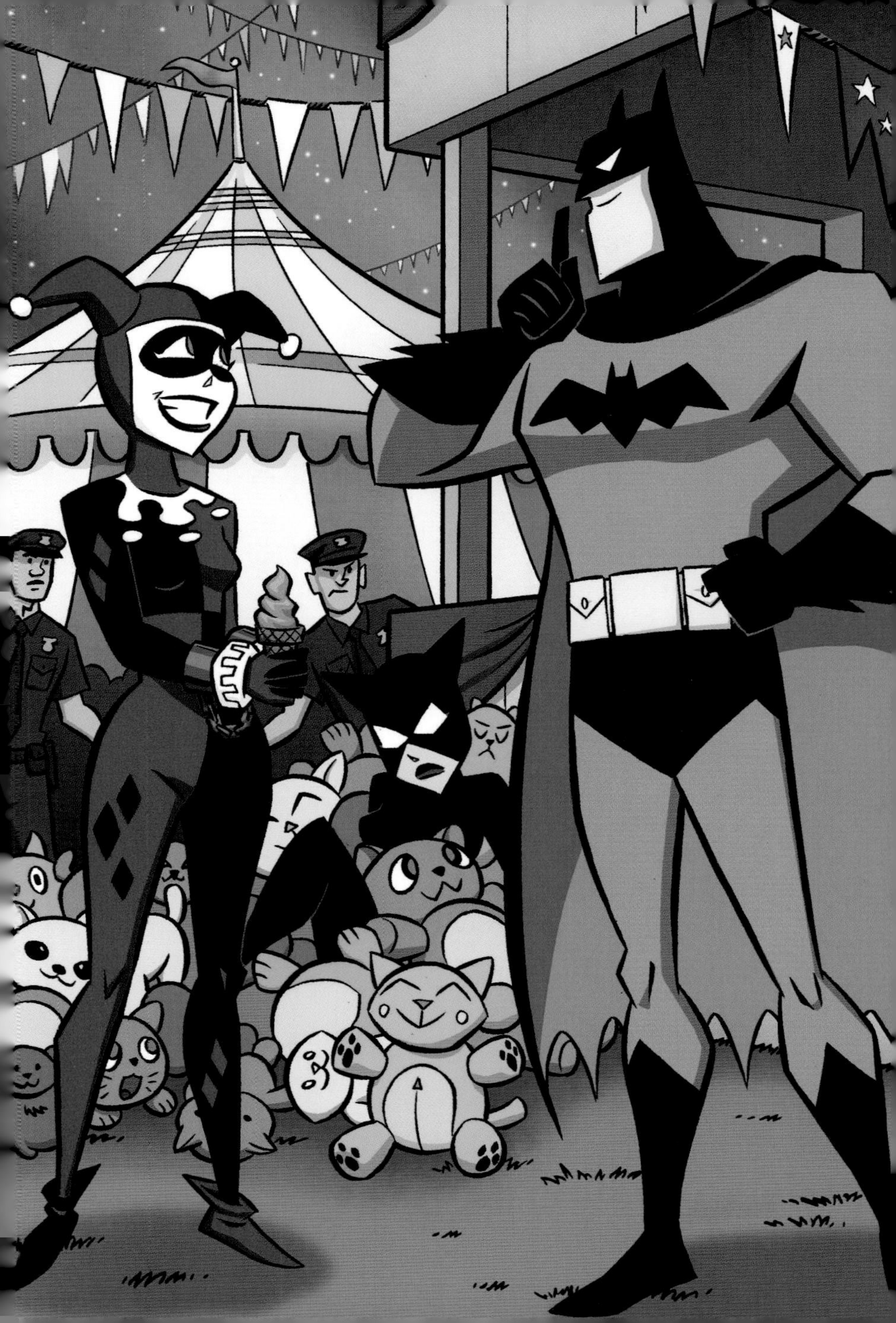

The Dark Knight concludes that Catwoman and Poison Ivy will go to Aqualandia Water Park. It's the next stop on the bus route, and he expects the female felons will jump off the first chance they get. Batman knows he has to get there, fast.

He starts to run down the street but doesn't go far. He stops at a parked limo and knocks on the driver's window. The window rolls down, and Alfred Pennyworth looks out.

"Open the trunk, Alfred," Batman says.

The loyal butler does as the Dark Knight asks, and Batman pulls out an odd-looking harness. He straps it on, pushes a button, and wings unfold.

"I'll be late getting home," he tells Alfred.

A small jet engine roars, and Batman launches into the night sky.

"I'll wait up for you, Master Bruce," Alfred replies as the Dark Knight flies away.

Batman soars over Gotham City. He spots the bus on the highway.

Catwoman and Ivy are still on the roof. The Dark Knight flies high above the vehicle, making sure the villainesses don't jump off. They don't. They ride on top of the bus all the way to the water park.

A lone passenger gets off the bus as it stops at Aqualandia. Batman sees that it's a night guard. The man doesn't notice Catwoman and Ivy jump off the roof of the bus behind him. Batman has never taken his eyes off the costumed criminals. He swoops down like a hawk and tosses a smoke capsule from his Utility Belt. *FWOOOOSH!*

Catwoman and Ivy are confused long enough for Batman to land and take off the Bat-Glider harness. He puts on a pair of thermal imaging goggles and runs into the smoke cloud to capture his foes.

Suddenly it's Batman's turn to be confused. The goggles are designed to pick up body heat. He should be able to see Catwoman and Poison Ivy as images of red and yellow warmth. There is no sign of them!

Turn the page.

The only heat the goggles pick up is too big to be human. Batman might not know what the object is, but he decides to lasso it with a Batrope.

A breeze blows away the smoke, and the Dark Knight sees what he has caught. It's a car! Not only that, the driver is Harley Quinn! Catwoman and Poison Ivy are inside the vehicle, protected from the smoke.

Batman doesn't know how Harley found her partners in crime or how she got here without him seeing her — especially in that weird-looking car. But that doesn't really matter now. Batman has other things to think about as the car starts to accelerate.

Turn to page 96.

Batman stands on a large tree branch and watches Ivy's green platform transform into a fanciful vine castle. A giant beanstalk sprouts at the base and lifts the structure into the sky. The stalk has thorns as big as elephant tusks!

"If I'm going to save that hostage, I'm going to have to climb that thing," the Dark Knight decides. "Just call me 'Jack.'"

The Dark Knight works his way down from the tree barrier and walks toward the enormous stem. It continues to grow taller and wider every second. Suddenly giant roots burst up out of the ground. They shoot up and then stab down into the soil. Batman has to jump aside to avoid them.

Again and again the Dark Knight has to leap and roll as the roots grow and spread. Finally he is close enough to the stalk to grab one of the giant thorns and use it like a handhold.

The Dark Knight pulls himself up onto the first spike. He looks up along the soaring stem.

Turn the page.

"One down, a thousand more to go," he says as he starts to climb.

Brambles and barbs growing on the stalk snag Batman's costume. The extra-strong material resists damage from the plant, but the offshoots act like tiny hands that grab him and slow him down. They are strong for their size.

"It's time to take the express," the Dark Knight says.

He takes his grapnel from his Utility Belt and fires it higher up the beanstalk.

THUNK! The grapnel takes hold on the giant stem. Batman gives the attached Batrope a tug to test it, then he swings out from the stalk in a wide arc. A gear on the grapnel pulls in the rope and tows Batman upward. He zooms past the brambles and barbs.

Nothing stops him until he gets to the top of the beanstalk. That's where he faces an unusual obstacle. The bottom of Ivy's castle is a wild tangle of vines and thorns where the stalk meets it. The mass looks like twisted barbed wire.

The Dark Knight reaches into his Utility Belt and pulls out a small canister. He breaks it on the surface of the beanstalk, and a freezing liquid splashes the stem. Ice forms and spreads along the thorny vines.

Batman uses a Batarang to break the frozen plants. He crawls up through the opening he has created and into Poison Ivy's stronghold.

Turn to page 99.

Batman studies the trail that heads to the right. It leads toward the main circus tent — the Big Top! He can hear the sounds of panic coming from that direction.

That's a sure sign that Harley Quinn is there!

The Dark Knight rushes to the Big Top. When he goes inside, he sees that it is a true three-ring circus. Harley drives her roller-coaster vehicle around and around the center ring. She's chasing a clown car full of clowns!

Catwoman is in the lion tamer's cage in a side ring. She's releasing the lions and tigers!

Batman fires his grapnel. It anchors on the support pole for the trapeze act in the center of the Big Top. The Dark Knight leaps and swings through the air toward Harley in the main ring.

Turn to page 94.

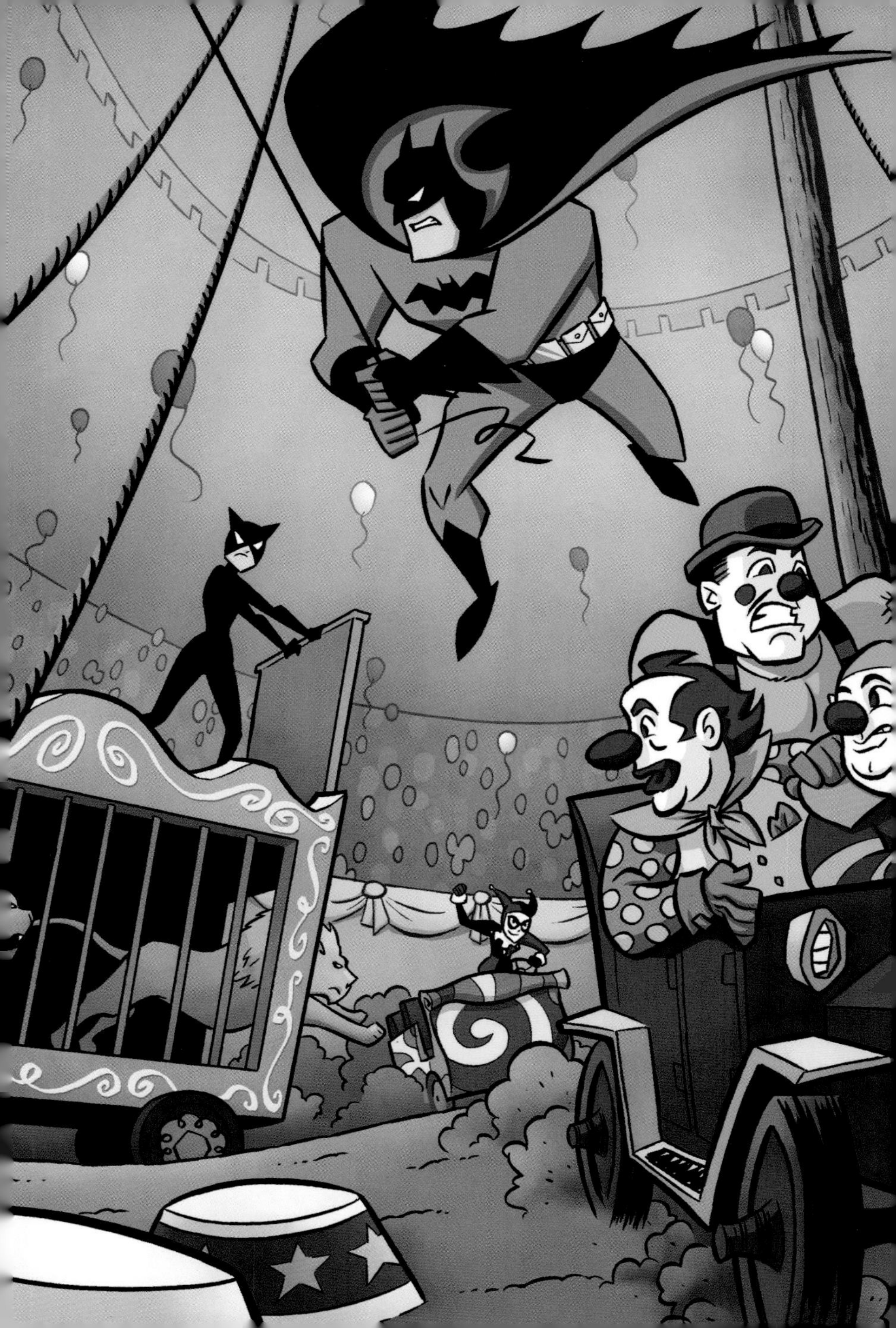

Catwoman catches a glance of the caped crime fighter as he swoops over her head. It's the last thing she notices. Batman takes a sleeping-gas capsule from his Utility Belt and tosses it to the ground. It erupts in a thick cloud. The lions and tigers yawn and lie down for a nice nap. Catwoman curls up with the big cats and goes to sleep, too.

Batman reaches the end of his swing on the Batrope and lets go. He drops down into the passenger seat of Harley Quinn's roller-coaster car!

"Yaaaa!" Harley shrieks in surprise.

Batman grabs the steering wheel and tries to keep the crazy car inside the circus ring. He needs to protect the performers and innocent audience members. Harley does not let go of the wheel. Neither does the Dark Knight. Both struggle for control of the car, which makes it go *out* of control!

Two dueling drivers are the same as none at all.

SMAAAASH! The vehicle crashes into the trapeze support pole. Harley leaps out of the vehicle and scampers up the ladder to the aerial platform. She grabs a trapeze bar and swings out. Then she swings back.

"Ooooh! This is nice . . ." Harley sighs as she goes back and forth above the Big Top. She hangs upside down by her knees, going nowhere.

"Well, that seems to amuse her," Batman observes.

The Dark Knight is ready to wrap up the case and take the female felons into custody.

"It's too bad that Poison Ivy escaped," he says.

A giant flower blossom bursts out of the ground in the center of the Big Top. It unfurls to reveal the Princess of Plants.

"Oh. There she is," Batman says.

Turn to page 103.

Harley Quinn steps on the gas, and her crazy car zooms toward the main gate of Aqualandia Water Park. The Batrope is still wrapped around the vehicle, and it snaps tight in Batman's grip. He is pulled forward, but the Dark Knight leaps up and over the car and lands on the hood.

THWUMP!

"Yaaaa!" Harley yells in surprise. She turns the steering wheel sharply. **SMAAAASH!** The car crashes through the gate.

"Yaaaa!" Catwoman and Ivy yell from the backseat.

Batman is silent as he hangs onto the hood.

The night guard finally notices the commotion and runs to the main security station. He turns on all the lights in the water park to see what's happening. He is amazed to see a clownish car speeding along the main boardwalk with Batman riding it like a wild bronco. The guard loses sight of the vehicle when it smashes into a gift shop.

Stuffed toys and souvenirs bounce off Batman and onto the windshield.

"I can't drive if I can't see where I'm going!" Harley complains.

"You can't drive in the first place!" Catwoman shouts.

Batman can see where Harley is headed. He leaps off the hood just before the car crashes into the checkout booth. **SMAAAASH!** Catwoman, Ivy, and Harley stumble out of the vehicle.

"Run!" Catwoman says.

"I'm trying," Harley moans as she wobbles a short distance and falls down.

The Dark Knight snaps Bat-cuffs on Harley's wrists and ankles. He runs after Catwoman and Poison Ivy. Again. They aren't hard to find. The water park is as bright as day. Batman isn't hard to miss, either.

Poison Ivy causes some stray weeds to grow to giant size and tangle the Dark Knight in their stems. Batman grabs a capsule of weed spray from his Utility Belt. **SPRIIIIZTTT!** The stalks shrivel and release him.

Turn the page.

Ivy tries to escape across an active kiddy ride. Seashell pods whirl gently. She is already dizzy from Harley's car ride and can't keep her balance.

"Ooh!" Ivy moans, collapsing.

Batman snaps Bat-cuffs on her and runs after Catwoman. He knows that the Cat Queen of Crime is as dizzy as Harley and Ivy. That fact gives him an idea. The Dark Knight chases the Feline Felon toward the merry-go-round.

"I might be dizzy, but I'm not stupid," Catwoman laughs at Batman as she realizes his plan. She swerves away from the carousel.

"Neither am I," Batman says.

The Dark Knight throws a Batarang, and it trips Catwoman. She falls straight into a giant box of beach sand. Suddenly she is surrounded by police. The night guard has called for backup!

"Thanks, Batman," says the officer in charge.

"All in a night's work," Batman replies.

THE END

To follow another path, turn to page 11.

Batman sees that he is in the middle of a royal throne room made of flowers. The walls are woven together from their stems, and bright blossoms hang like lights from the ceiling. At one end of the grand room is a throne constructed of giant roses. Poison Ivy sits in the fabulous chair like a queen.

"It seems I have an intruder in my realm," Ivy observes.

"Throw him in the dungeon with that other guy," Harley Quinn suggests. She juggles bunches of bouquets next to Ivy's throne.

"Oh no, my dear Court Jester. I have another plan for the Dark Knight," declares the Queen of Green.

Suddenly the walls of the chamber start to move. They shift backward to make the room wider. Something starts to grow up from the floor. Batman puts his hands on his Utility Belt, ready for anything.

A part of the main beanstalk rises and twists to form a medieval knight.

Turn the page.

"Behold my Green Knight!" Poison Ivy announces. "He will do battle with the Dark Knight to win the freedom of the hostage."

"Um, don't knights usually fight over a girl? The hostage is a guy," Harley points out, confused.

"Minor detail," Ivy shrugs. "Let the games begin!"

The Green Knight raises his sword and attacks Batman. The Caped Crusader sees that the knight is attached to the main beanstalk and is sure he can easily dodge the threat, but small vines suddenly wrap around his ankles.

He can't move! He reaches for his Utility Belt.

SNIIIK! The sharp points of a Batarang slice through the thin vines.

The Dark Knight throws the Batarang at the Green Knight and cuts the plant sword in half.

SHIIIING! A new one forms. The Green Knight charges Batman again!

Turn to page 102.

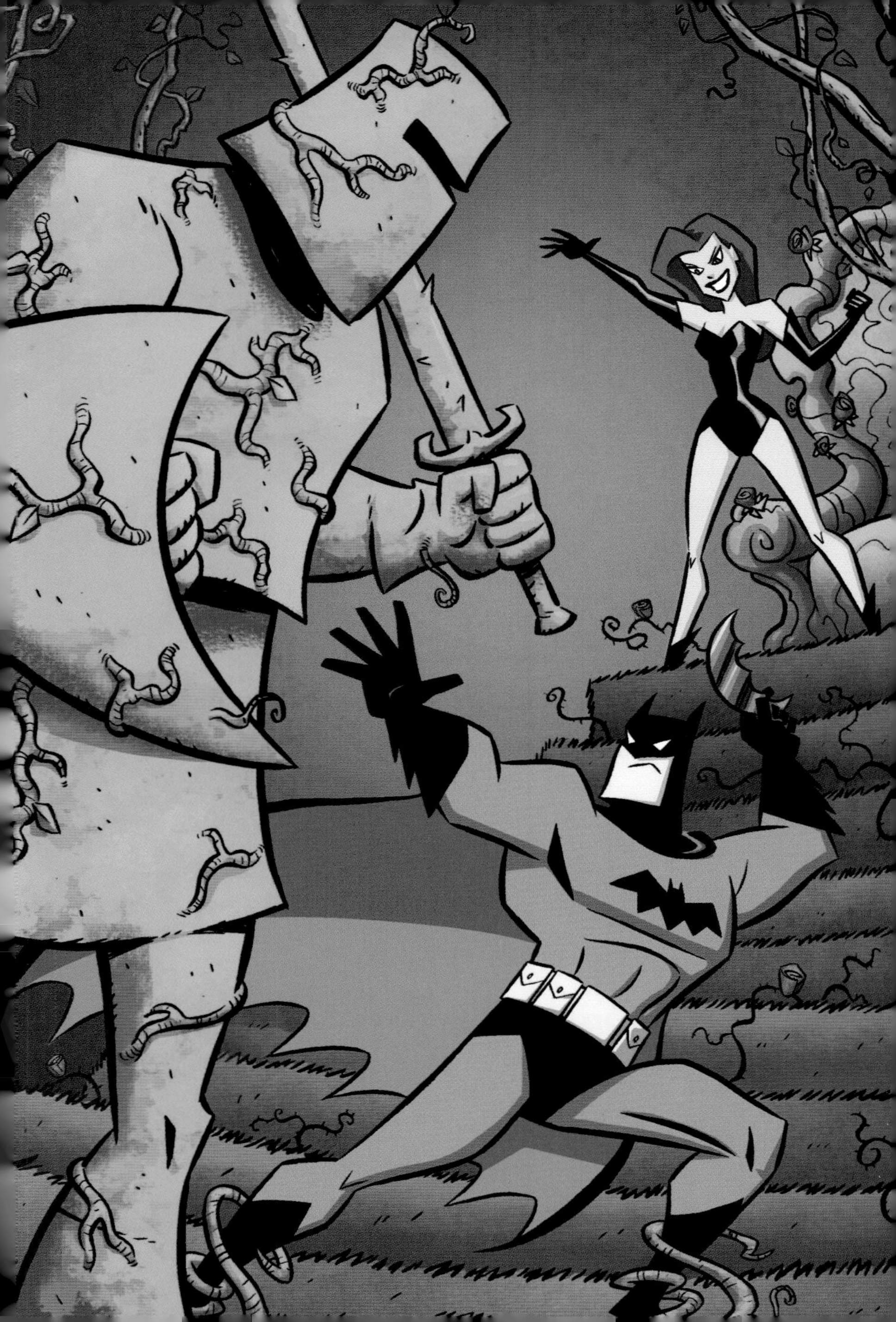

Batman doesn't try to dodge the Green Knight this time. He runs straight toward him.

"What's he doing?" Ivy gasps.

"He's crazier than I am!" Harley declares.

The Dark Knight jumps over the Green Knight and his horse like a trick rider at a rodeo. At the same time, he reaches toward his Utility Belt. **PWOOOOF!** A cloud of sleeping gas blooms around Ivy and Harley. They drop to the flowery floor instantly. The vine castle starts to untangle. The beanstalk shrinks. It only takes a few minutes for Ivy's empire to fall apart. Gotham Park goes back to normal.

"It looks like Ivy and Harley slept through their defeat and capture," Commissioner Gordon tells Batman as the felons are taken away and the hostage climbs into an ambulance.

"That's a good idea," the Dark Knight says, and he heads home to bed!

THE END

To follow another path, turn to page 11.

The enormous bloom grows up out of the ground in the middle of the Big Top. It opens, and there is Poison Ivy standing inside like a Queen on her throne. Batman watches her blow kisses at the cheering audience. They think it is part of the show. The Dark Knight knows better!

"She's exhaling mind-control spores," he realizes.

Batman pulls a special filter mask from his Utility Belt and places it over his nose and mouth. It protects him as the spores float over him and the nearby circus performers. Suddenly the performers straighten up like soldiers at attention. They all look toward Poison Ivy and wait for orders. She points at Batman.

"Attack," Ivy commands.

The enslaved performers rush toward the Dark Knight. The acrobats do cartwheels and handsprings at incredible speed!

"These guys are good," Batman admits. "So am I."

Turn the page.

The Dark Knight is trained in acrobatic arts and martial skills. Instead of bracing for a defensive fight, he decides to take the battle to his foes. Batman runs straight toward the frontrunner of the acrobatic assault!

The Caped Crusader uses an ankle kick to trip the leader and then leaps onto his back. He uses the performer like a springboard to launch himself over the rest of the acrobats and flip over their heads. He lands on top of the giant metal hoop called the Wheel of Steel!

"This isn't your average seesaw," Batman declares as he tries to find his balance.

Vines from Ivy's plant reach out and tug sharply at the Wheel of Steel. Batman is thrown off the hoop and goes flying through the air! He uses his cape to guide his flight. *WHAAAM!* He smashes directly into the giant flower.

Poison Ivy is knocked out of her blossom and into the circus sawdust. She looks up at Batman for a moment as he floats down like a dark dandelion puff.

A moment later, she falls unconscious and her mind control is broken. The acrobats stop in their tracks.

Batman stands in the middle of the circus Big Top. Catwoman sleeps with the big cats. Poison Ivy sprawls in the sawdust. Harley Quinn swings upside down on the trapeze.

"The circus is saved!" someone yells. The audience roars with cheers and applause.

The circus ringmaster rushes up and shakes Batman's hand.

"Thank you for saving my show!" the man says. "You have fantastic skills! Let me know if you ever want to join my circus. You gave me a great idea for an act!"

THE END

To follow another path, turn to page 11.

AUTHOR

Laurie S. Sutton has read comics since she was a kid.
She grew up to become an editor for Marvel, DC Comics,
Starblaze, and Tekno Comics. She has written Adam
Strange for DC, Star Trek: Voyager for Marvel, plus Star
Trek: Deep Space Nine and Witch Hunter for Malibu
Comics. There are long boxes of comics in her closet where
there should be clothing and shoes. Laurie has lived all over
the world, and currently resides in Florida.

ILLUSTRATOR

Ethen Beavers is a professional comic book artist from
Modesto, California. His best-known works for DC Comics
include Justice League Unlimited and Legion of Superheroes
in the 31st Century. He has also illustrated for other top
publishers, including Marvel, Dark Horse, and Abrams.

GLOSSARY

archenemy (arch-EN-uh-mee)—one's main or principle foe

asylum (uh-SYE-lum)—a hospital for people who are mentally ill and cannot live by themselves

Batarang (BAT-uh-rayng)—a sharp, metal throwing weapon used by Batman

endangered (en-DAYN-jurd)—threatened with extinction, such as a rare species of plant or animal

felon (FEL-uhn)—one who has committed a serious crime punishable by a heavy sentence

hypnotized (HIP-nuh-tized)—deadened the judgment or resistance by or as if by hypnotic suggestion

mayhem (MAY-hem)—needless or willful damage or violence

tendrils (TEN-druhlz)— a slender, leafless winding stem by which some climbing plants fasten themselves to a support

Utility Belt (yoo-TIL-uh-tee BELT)—Batman's belt, which holds all of his weaponry and gadgets

POISON IVY

Real Name:
Pamela Isley

Occupation:
Professional Criminal,
Botanist

Base:
Gotham City

Height:
5 feet 6 inches

Weight:
110 lbs.

Eyes:
Green

Hair:
Chestnut

CATWOMAN

Real Name:
Selina Kyle

Occupation:
Professional Thief

Base:
Gotham City

Height:
5 feet 7 inches

Weight:
125 lbs.

Eyes:
Green

Hair:
Black

HARLEY QUINN

Real Name:
Dr. Harleen Quinzel

Occupation:
Professional
Criminal

Base:
Gotham City

Height:
5 feet 7 inches

Weight:
140 lbs.

Eyes:
Blue

Hair:
Blonde

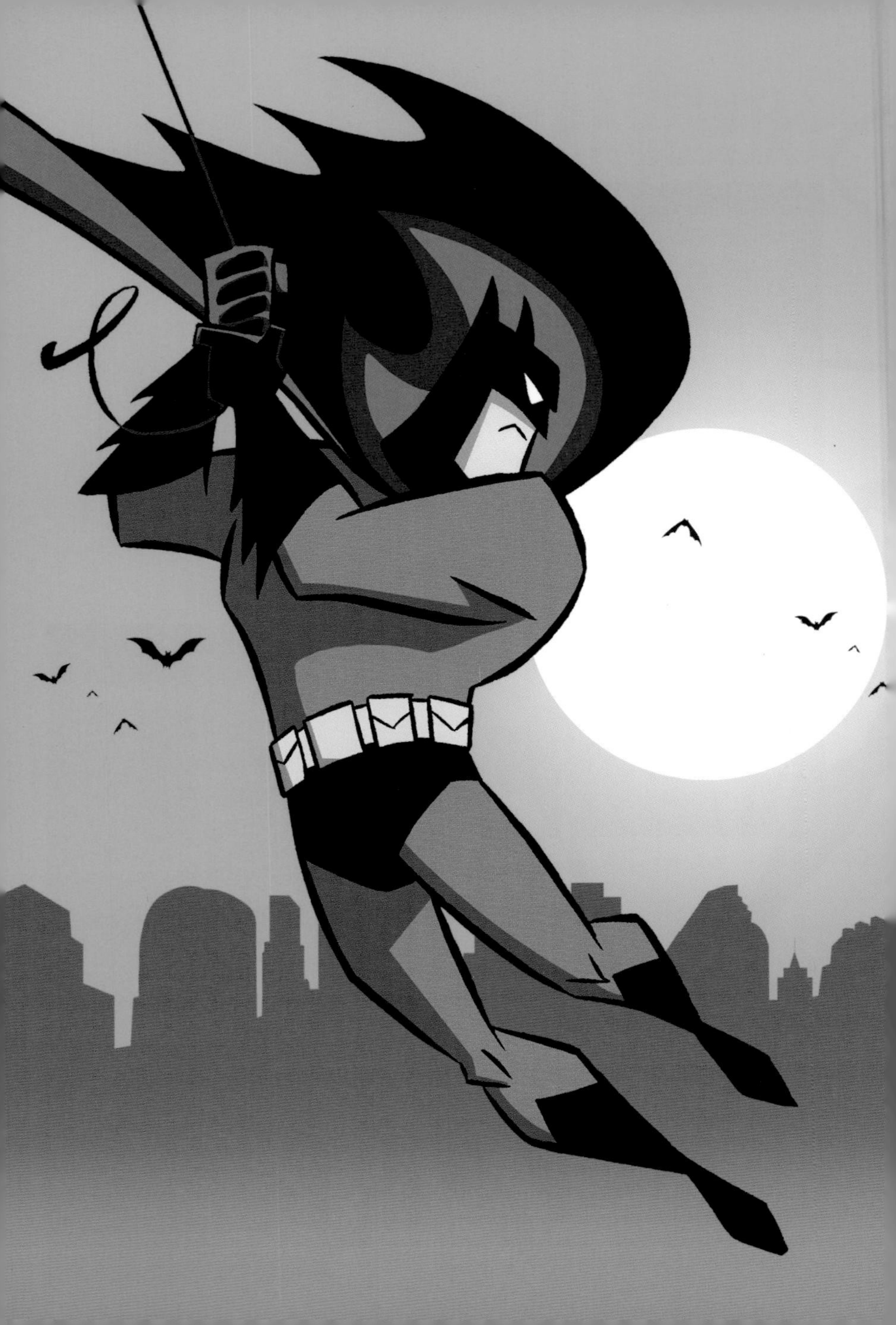

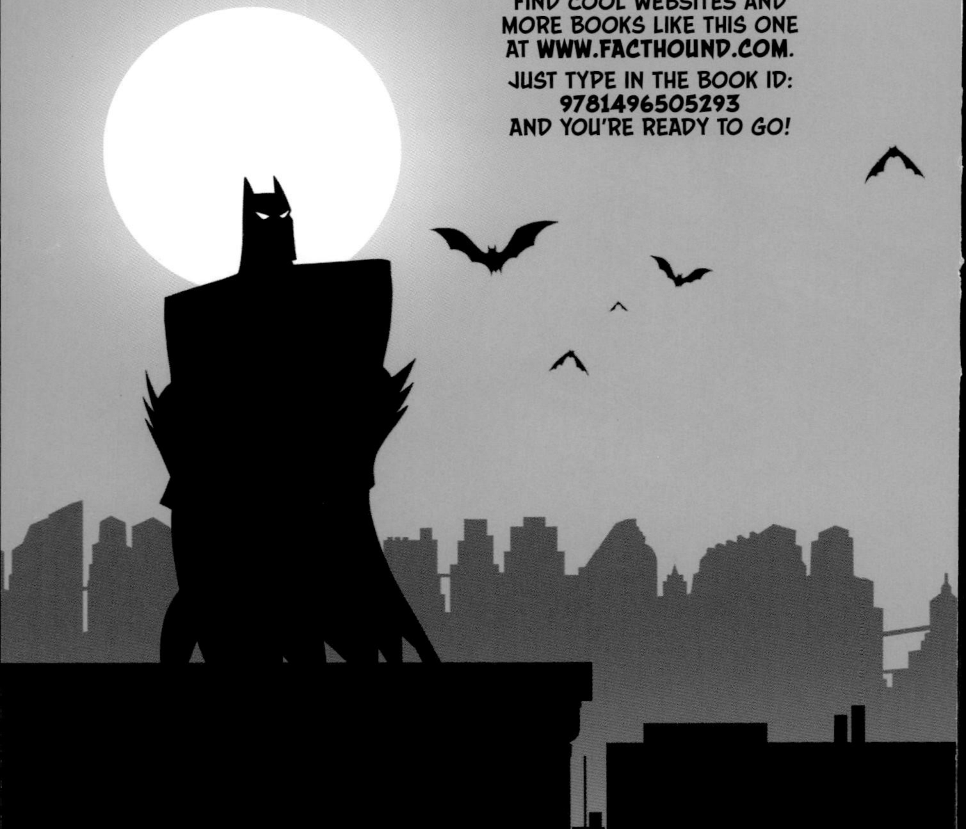

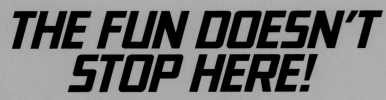